Secondhand Dogs

Secondhand Dogs

 CAROLYN CRIMI

Illustrated by Melissa Manwill

BALZER + BRAY

An Imprint of HarperCollinsPublishers

Balzer + Bray is an imprint of HarperCollins Publishers.

Secondhand Dogs
Text copyright © 2021 by Carolyn Crimi
Illustrations copyright © 2021 by Melissa Manwill

ISBN 978-0-06-298918-5

Typography by Molly Fehr
21 22 23 24 25   PC/LSCH   10 9 8 7 6 5 4 3 2 1

First Edition

For Stephanie, who believed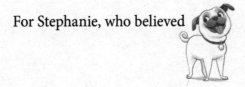

Gus

Gus lifted his head and sniffed the chilly November air. The smell of dead leaves wafted through the windows and into the cramped kitchen. Someone a few houses down had a fire burning in their fireplace, and that smell, too, curled its way inside.

Gus sat on his bed. The tip of his tail nervously flipped up and down as he watched Miss Lottie gather the things she liked to bring to the dog park—sodas, snacks, treats, beach towels, food bowls.

Miss Lottie only took them to the dog park when she was introducing a new dog to the pack. It was neutral territory, since it wasn't their home and it wasn't the new dog's home, either. She would pick up Quinn, the eleven-year-old neighbor who helped her out, and drive him and the dogs to the park. After they were settled, she would bring the new dog over for a meet 'n' greet.

As he watched Miss Lottie, Gus felt a strange tremble in his gut. He'd had it all morning. Since he was the first dog Miss Lottie had adopted, under Dog Pack Law he was now the pack leader, which meant it was his responsibility to keep everyone safe and happy. So far he had managed to do that, but a new dog could change everything.

"New member," said Tank. The big bulldog spoke to Gus using the usual animal language of snorts, sniffs, scratches, blinks, and grunts.

"Looks that way," Gus said.

"It'll be great," Tank said. "It always is."

Easy for Tank to say. He wasn't the leader. He didn't have to introduce a nervous new dog to the pack. He didn't have to make sure a fight didn't break out. He didn't have to give his official approval of the new dog.

Roo got up from her dog bed, did a quick spin, then sat back down. Her ears twitched.

"New dog day," Roo said to Gus. She did another spin.

"I hope it's a puppy!" said Moon Pie. The one-year-old pug wandered over to Tank and snuggled next to him.

"I hope it's *not* a puppy," Roo said. She scratched an ear. "Puppies make me nervous."

"Everything makes you nervous," Tank said.

A puppy would be a different kind of challenge. Puppies meant lots of messes and playful nips with needle-sharp teeth. Puppies needed a strong leader to show them the proper way to behave. Even Moon Pie, who was just out of puppyhood, could be a handful at times.

"Today's the day, kiddos!" Miss Lottie said. She ushered the dogs out to the driveway, where her rusty, dented van sat. She pulled out the special ramp that made it easier for the dogs, especially the older ones like Roo and Tank, to climb inside.

As the leader, Gus was expected to go first.

Gus hesitated. The strange tremble in his gut worried him. He had never felt this way about a new dog's arrival before.

"Come on, come on, WE'RE WAITING!" Roo snapped.

"Right." Gus ran up the ramp and gave himself a shake before sitting by the window. That feeling in his gut was probably just the rock he ate earlier. He had a bad habit of eating things that weren't food.

"Geez, took ya long enough," Roo said as she wedged herself in next to him.

"I was thinking," Gus said.

"Uh-huh," Roo said.

Roo was often annoyed with Gus. His indecisiveness made her more anxious than she already was. Roo wanted answers. Fast action. Quick decisions.

Gus wasn't very good at any of those things.

When they arrived at Quinn's house, he was waiting out front. Miss Lottie never had to honk her horn for Quinn.

He was always waiting there, looking as though his life depended on the van taking him away. Gus often wondered why.

"It's a big day!" Miss Lottie said.

Quinn smiled, eyes downcast, as he quickly climbed into the van.

"Hey, everyone," he said in his soft voice. He turned to the back seat and gave each dog a pat on the head.

Gus licked Quinn's hand. Even though Quinn wasn't technically part of the pack, Gus felt responsible for him. Quinn was a good belly rubber and an excellent chin scratcher. On days like today, when Quinn seemed sad, Gus would spend more time than usual nuzzling him or curling up on his lap. Sometimes it worked. Sometimes it didn't.

"You'll love the new dog," Miss Lottie said.

"Boy or girl?" Quinn asked.

"It's a secret," Miss Lottie said.

"Big or little?"

"I'm not telling!" Miss Lottie laughed. "Don't you like surprises? I do."

Quinn didn't reply. He slid his phone out and started reading his texts.

"You sure do get a lot of texts," Miss Lottie said.

Quinn shrugged. "I guess," he said.

Gus watched trees zoom by as the old van made its way to the dog park. He couldn't shake the bad feeling. Maybe it was the tennis ball he had eaten yesterday. Tennis balls were especially hard to digest.

"We're here!" said Miss Lottie.

The dog park was empty, the weather too cold and gray for most people. The large, fenced-in lot was mostly dirt with a few patches of grass and a handful of benches facing every which way, as though they had been tossed there by a giant storm and never put back in the proper place. A tangle of trees sat in the corner.

The pack tumbled through the gate. They stood near Quinn and waited patiently as he spread out the beach towels and set up the folding chairs.

"I'll be right back," Miss Lottie called from the van.

Quinn gave her a small wave and sat on a chair. He patted his lap. Moon Pie danced over to him, yipped, then danced away. Typical Moon Pie.

"Silly little guy." Quinn grinned.

Moon Pie was both the youngest and the smallest member of the pack and had only been at Miss Lottie's for a month. Everyone was already attached to him, especially Tank.

"This looks like a good spot," Tank said. He spread out on a beach towel and started licking his big belly.

"Do you ever STOP?" Roo asked.

"Nope," Tank said. He turned around and started licking the other side.

It was quite a thing to behold, Tank's stomach. Big and

perfectly round. When he had first arrived, it had been mostly pink, but it had changed over the years, the way all old dogs' bellies change, with dark, bumpy growths pushing up through his fur. It didn't matter. He still licked and licked and licked.

Roo made small circles in the grass, trying to find the perfect spot to lie down.

"Can't get comfortable! Just can't, JUST CAN'T!"

She never could. Maybe it was because she had three legs instead of four, or maybe it was because of her nervous disposition. Whatever it was, Roo, the only hunting dog in the pack, was a quivering bundle of barking, running energy. She was nine, so she was a year older than Tank and two years older than Gus, but her jumpiness made her seem younger than both of them. Today she was squirmier than usual.

Gus rested his chin on Quinn's leg. Quinn started scratching behind Gus's ears.

Gus sighed. Quinn's ear rubs always made him feel better. Maybe everything would be okay. All he had to do was make sure this dog was a good addition to the pack. If he was, Gus would give his official wag and his small woof. If he wasn't, well, Gus would have to think about that. It had never happened before.

The shelter wasn't far from the dog park. Soon Miss Lottie was pulling back into the parking lot.

"They're here," Quinn said.

They all watched as Miss Lottie got out of the van. She smoothed her gray, frizzy hair and looked up at the sky.

"Looks like a storm's coming," she said to Quinn. She hitched up her pants and opened the back door. A large dog hopped out. A dog who did not need the ramp.

A breeze brushed past. Gus stood. He sniffed the air.

Something smelled off.

Way off.

Gus

The new dog walked calmly next to Miss Lottie. His ears and his tail were both up. Alert, but not alarmed.

He wasn't nervous. Not like the other dogs had been when they first approached the pack.

He was sizing them up, Gus decided. Gus didn't know what to think about that. Usually new dogs pulled back a bit, or wiggled a little too much, or stood their ground and barked.

Not this dog.

Gus sniffed the air again. The scent that wafted off the new dog was bright and cold, like the metal water bowl in Miss Lottie's kitchen.

Gus had always hated that bowl.

"Meet Decker, everyone!" said Miss Lottie.

Decker sat on his haunches. He was sleek and muscular, with a long, sharp nose and dark, shiny fur. He glanced at the pack with pale eyes, then stared off into the distance.

"He looks . . . confident," Quinn said. He had stopped scratching Gus behind the ears.

Miss Lottie grunted when her bottom hit her beach chair, just like her old dogs did when they flopped down on their beds.

"Probably just bluffing," Miss Lottie said. She stroked Decker's coat with her palm. "Isn't he a beauty? He reminds me of Mr. Beans, the very first dog I had when I was little." She sighed and shook her head. "Mr. Beans was such a great dog. And this guy looks just like him!" Her smile took up her whole face as she gazed at the new dog. "I figure he's part shepherd, part husky. Maybe a little Doberman, too."

Gus rooted around until he found a rock to gnaw on. If Miss Lottie liked Decker, he must be okay. She wouldn't introduce a new dog into the pack if she thought he was bad.

Tank struggled to stand. "Don't like the smell of this one," he said. "He won't make a good pack member, Gus!"

"Why aren't they sniffing him?" Quinn asked.

"I don't know," Miss Lottie said. "Gus, how do you like Decker?"

The sick feeling in Gus's stomach was back, and it wasn't from a rock or a tennis ball. It was the uncertainty of how to respond to the new dog that was making him nauseous. He had to do something, but what?

"Is he our new member, huh, Gus? Is he, is he?" Roo asked. She started her sharp staccato barks.

Moon Pie gave a happy yap and trotted over to the new dog in his puppylike way.

"Hello! I'm Moon Pie!" he said. "I'm only here for a little while, since I'll be going back to my human soon. Right, Gus?"

There it was again. The question Gus dreaded answering. Moon Pie had asked a few times before, and so far Gus had managed to ignore him. Gus glanced over at Tank, but Tank was focused on the new dog.

"I don't like the way he's looking at Moon Pie!" Tank said. He glared at Decker as he said it, daring him to speak.

"Give him a chance, Tank," Gus said.

But he had noticed it, too. There was a strange glint in the new dog's eyes.

"Look at his beautiful coat," Miss Lottie said. She rubbed one of Decker's ears between her fingers. "It's just gorgeous. And he's so calm! I'm telling you, Quinn, it's like my Mr. Beans all over again!"

"Is he in or out, Gus? In or out!" Roo barked and ran in furious little circles. She did this when she was upset, which was often. "I HATE not knowing!"

"Roo," Quinn said. He leaned over and grabbed her

by the collar before she could run another loop. "Shh. It's okay. Shhhhh."

Roo panted heavily. "He seems okay, but what do I know? I'm not the leader! Make up your mind, Gus!"

"I'm thinking!" Gus said.

"You're always thinking!" Roo said.

"Why doesn't he say something?" Tank asked. "He's just sitting there like—"

Like he's the leader of the pack, Gus thought.

He strode over to Decker and stood before him. "We're a good pack," Gus said. "We won't bite, as the humans say."

"Really?" Decker said. He looked Gus squarely in the eyes. "Well, I can't promise the same."

"What?" Gus asked. His heartbeat quickened.

"Just kidding. I only bite food." Decker licked his lips, showing long, sharp teeth.

"That's funny!" Roo said. "He's funny, Gus! Is he in?"

Gus's deep-down dogginess, his gut instincts, could not give approval to this new dog. It felt as wrong and as bad as letting a wolf into the pack.

Gus would have to growl. Snarl, even. Somehow he would let Miss Lottie know that this new dog was not okay.

Miss Lottie kissed Decker on top of his head.

"Mr. Beans was the sweetest thing," she said to Quinn. "If I was ever worried about something, he would lick my hand. And you're the same, aren't you, buddy?"

The new dog turned to her. Gus watched in amazement as he inched in, then leaned over and licked her hand.

"Oh, now, see that?" Miss Lottie laughed. "It's like he IS Mr. Beans!"

"He's bad, Gus! Don't let him in!" Tank said.

"He's fine!" Roo said. "Let him in, Gus, let him in!"

Roo started to howl. Tank barked so vigorously that his front feet left the ground. Moon Pie simply stared up at the new dog, who was easily four times his size.

Gus had always had good feelings about the other dogs soon after he met them. Always. Decker was the first who smelled and acted wrong.

But what if Gus's deep-down dogginess was off? Roo didn't have a problem with the new dog. Moon Pie seemed okay with him, too.

"Gus, what are you going to DO?" asked Roo.

Maybe this new dog just needed a chance, like Miss Lottie was always saying. And if Gus didn't give his approval, what would happen to Decker? If Miss Lottie sensed they weren't getting along, she might take him back to the shelter. What if no one ever adopted him? Gus didn't think he could live with that.

He wished he had more time to make this decision. To carefully weigh each and every option.

"What a good boy," Miss Lottie said as she scratched Decker under the chin.

And so Gus did it. He gave the small woof and the wag, his official sign of approval.

Roo and Tank stopped barking. Moon Pie plopped down next to Dexter.

"They seem okay now," Miss Lottie said. She looked up at the low clouds. "Do you feel rain?"

"Yup," Quinn said.

Gus saw a flash of lightning in the distance. Roo whined.

"Oh well. Guess it's time for home already," Miss Lottie said.

She and Quinn loaded the beach chairs, the towels, and the cooler into the van.

"Okay, kiddos, all in!" Miss Lottie said.

The dogs jogged over. They stood by the back door while Miss Lottie pulled out the ramp.

Gus was waiting for the ramp to be put in place when suddenly he felt a hard ball of fur and bone thud against his side.

"Oof!" Gus lost his balance and fell into a crumpled heap. Dazed, he looked up.

Decker wagged his tail and hopped into the van.

First.

Gus got to his feet as quickly as he could. He ran up the ramp with all the energy he had left after the stressful afternoon.

But it was too late. Miss Lottie was already in the van, so

she hadn't seen. Quinn, who was in charge of putting the ramp back after they were all in, was checking his phone again.

But his pack had seen what happened. They had seen the new dog enter the van first, as if he were the leader. He was challenging Gus, and the pack knew it.

Gus worried for the rest of the ride. Being a good leader meant taking control of new situations. If the other dogs thought Decker might suddenly become their leader, they'd worry about their own places in the pack.

He had to keep everyone happy. He couldn't let another pack down.

Gus Before

When Gus was a puppy, he always woke up with the mother. She would take him for his walks in gray weather and in bright weather and in snow-white weather. She would talk to him about her upcoming day and hurry him up, just a little, while he did his business.

When the boy came home, he would take Gus to the park where they watched the ducks swim in the pond.

In the afternoon, Gus would wait by the front door to greet the father with a happy bark. The big man always rubbed the top of Gus's head before walking into the house.

He loved his pack, and his pack loved him.

They were messy cooks, which made Gus happy, since they often let meaty scraps fall to the floor. Gus was happiest, though, when they were all together watching TV. He would go from lap to lap to lap all night.

The days melted into each other. Walks, park, head rub, dinner, TV. Walks, park, head rub, dinner, TV. The sameness was comforting to Gus.

Until things changed. Gus wasn't sure exactly when it began. But the mother started hurrying Gus too much on his walk.

The boy stayed in his room in the afternoons.

The father sometimes forgot to rub Gus's head.

They didn't cook together. They didn't watch TV together. Sometimes they even snapped at him. For barking. For begging. For just being a dog.

Gus would wander from room to room to hop on laps, hoping that his presence would comfort them, but it wasn't the same.

He tried everything in his power to make them happy. He brought tennis balls to the boy and a pair of old socks to the father. He didn't eat the bacon off the table, even when the mother placed a plate of it achingly close to the edge. He barked less, wagged more, and always did what he was told. He was sure that if he could just be a better dog, maybe they would be happy again.

It didn't work, and one day the mother and the boy left.

The father stayed with Gus, but he had changed. He slept in front of the TV. He yelled into the phone. He fed Gus and walked him, but other than that, he ignored him.

So when the father left the back gate open, Gus walked through it. He paused on the other side, seeing if the father would notice. He didn't. Gus kept going.

Gus hoped his old family would come together as they looked for him. He hoped they'd be so happy to have him home that they'd go back to living their old life as a pack, as a family.

He walked and he walked until he came to the park. He sat on the grass near the pond and watched the ducks until it grew dark, then he curled up in the grass and slept. He stayed there for days, gnawing on a rock. His stomach grumbled, but he didn't move. Surely his family would come looking for him.

Then someone did come. A large woman with frizzy hair wandered across the park and sat next to him.

"You look like you could use a friend," she said.

She coaxed him into her van, which sparkled like the pond in the morning sun. She fixed him his very own dinner and watched TV with him.

She made phone calls about him and put up signs about the sweet and scruffy terrier she had found. But the family never came.

There were no other dogs at Miss Lottie's back then. And while he loved Miss Lottie fiercely, his tiny pack of two could sometimes be lonely. At his old house, there was always someone around when he wanted to play or snuggle, but now, whenever Miss Lottie left, all he had were his tennis balls.

And so every day, as he went on walks and gnawed on rocks, Gus wished for a new dog. With each wish, he made a promise to himself that if he became part of a pack again, he would keep them together no matter what.

Quinn

Quinn sat in the front seat of the van with Moon Pie in his lap and watched the windshield wipers flick back and forth.

"Sure is coming down," Miss Lottie said. "Looks like my house will smell like wet dog for a while." She chuckled. "Not that it doesn't smell like that all the time."

"I kind of like that smell," Quinn said.

Miss Lottie smiled. "Me, too, actually. Smells like home."

Quinn turned to look at the dogs behind him. Roo's ears twitched. Gus and Tank both watched the new dog. Decker gazed out the window, ignoring them.

Quinn frowned. They were too quiet. Usually Roo barked at cars, and Tank would growl at her. But today they were both silent.

Moon Pie pawed at Quinn's shoulder.

"We're almost home, Moonie," Quinn said.

"I think he's hungry," Miss Lottie said. "I bet they all are, especially Decker. We'll need to fatten him up."

Decker did look lean, but a few weeks at Miss Lottie's would change that.

"Is he on any kind of special food or medication?" Quinn asked. A big part of his job at Miss Lottie's was giving the dogs their pills and eye drops. He loved doing it, and Miss Lottie loved that she didn't have to.

"Nope, he's totally healthy," Miss Lottie said. "Aren't you, Decker?"

Quinn glanced behind him. Decker stared at Miss Lottie for a moment, then went back to gazing out the window.

"Something got into the garbage last night," Miss Lottie said. "Probably raccoons. I'm going to have to start putting bricks on top of the lids again."

"They got into ours, too," Quinn said.

He didn't mention the conversation he had had with his mom. She had seen a coyote in the alley the night before. Quinn knew if Miss Lottie heard that, she wouldn't stop worrying about her dogs, so he decided to keep it to himself.

He took his phone out and, with a shaky hand, started scrolling through the texts that had accumulated in the short time he had been away from home. He counted three new ones from Cole and Sam, his brother's friends. They were texts about the way Quinn wore his hair, the way he walked, the way he talked. Nothing he did was okay.

"I know I just brought Moon Pie home a month ago, but I couldn't resist Decker," Miss Lottie said. "I hope they all get along."

"You've never had a problem before, have you?" Quinn asked. He frowned at his phone.

Miss Lottie nodded thoughtfully. "You're right, I haven't. It'll be fine."

Quinn's stomach clenched every time he read the texts, but he kept on doing it. If he could just understand why they'd chosen him as their target, then maybe he could change himself somehow.

Quinn knew, too, that he read all the texts hoping that someday his brother would jump in and defend him. Quinn could see that Jessie had read them, but he never responded to them, except for the occasional thumbs up.

And, of course, Jessie had been the one to give Cole and Sam Quinn's number in the first place. When they were bored and just hanging out, Jessie might even encourage them to text. Quinn often wondered if he did.

Miss Lottie pulled up to Quinn's house.

"Hey, there's Jessie!" she said. She waved enthusiastically at Quinn's brother, who was sitting on the front porch swing, tossing a baseball from one hand to the other. Jessie gave her an equally enthusiastic smile and waved back.

"It's so nice that he waits for you every day," Miss Lottie said.

Quinn slid out of the van.

"See you tomorrow?" Miss Lottie asked.

"Yup," he said.

"Great! The dogs always look forward to seeing you. Me, too, of course!"

She pulled away. Quinn kept his head down as he walked up the front steps. It was Friday, which meant macaroni and cheese from a box for dinner.

"Hey," Quinn mumbled as he passed Jessie.

"Hang on a second," Jessie said.

Quinn paused but kept his eyes on the porch floor, his heart hammering in his chest. Jessie rarely spoke to him these days.

"You are the worst person to be working with that weird old lady and her dogs. You know that, don't you? I can't believe she hired you to take care of them. Especially after what you did to Murph."

The words stung. Even though it had happened months ago, he still felt like crying every time he thought of their old dog, Murph. Jessie seemed to know that. He commented on how bad Quinn was with dogs whenever Quinn came home from Miss Lottie's.

Just like with the texts, it was best to suck it up and keep quiet. Maybe, after a while, Jessie and the others would get bored of bullying him. If he could hang on until then, everything would be all right.

Besides, Miss Lottie always told him he was good with the dogs. She said he was the best thing to happen to them since Tiddle Widdle Chicken Bits.

The door swung open. Quinn's mom stuck her head out.

"You're home! Want to help me with dinner? I could use your special touch with the orange powder." She gave Quinn a big grin. "You, too, Jessie! You can microwave the broccoli and melt the butter."

"Sure, Mom," Jessie said. He stood and gave Quinn a playful punch. "Come on, bro! Let's get cooking!"

As he walked into the house, Quinn felt a hard shove from behind.

"Moron," Jessie whispered.

Quinn stumbled but kept walking. He had to show Jessie how tough he was, how he could take it.

Quinn already couldn't wait until morning, when he could go back to Miss Lottie's. No one there cared if he was tough or cool.

Gus

Every dog had a dog gift, and Moon Pie's dog gift was begging.

Gus had noticed it from the first moment Moon Pie stepped into Miss Lottie's. It was inspiring, really, to watch Moon Pie in action.

"There he goes," Tank said. His gaze went from Moon Pie to the new dog, then back to Moon Pie.

"He's a pro, a real pro!" Roo said. She was sitting on her bed. She, too, kept shifting her gaze to the new dog.

Decker sat near the back door, quiet and still. Gus kept glancing over at him, but Decker barely moved.

Moon Pie was the only one who seemed oblivious to the tension in the kitchen. He was completely focused on Miss Lottie and the pork on the cutting board.

Miss Lottie liked to sing as she cooked. Tonight she was singing along to a slow, soft song playing on her iPod. Her large hips swooshed back and forth. Every once in a while, she tilted her head back and belted out one long, loud note. This always made Roo howl.

"Sing it, Roo, sing it!" Miss Lottie cried.

Roo howled louder.

Gus wagged his tail. He loved it when Miss Lottie sang.

Keeping a close eye on Miss Lottie's feet, Moon Pie took two dainty steps toward her.

Miss Lottie started. "Oh, Moon Pie, I didn't see you!" she said, looking down at the little dog. "Don't get underfoot, now."

But that was precisely what Moon Pie did so well. He got underfoot without getting hurt. Miss Lottie would take a step in one direction and Moon Pie would take a step in the same direction. His tiny paw would only be a hair's width away from Miss Lottie's big foot.

Miss Lottie turned and shook her head. "Now, now," she said. She reached down to pet Moon Pie, who somehow was able to make his eyes bigger and rounder than any other dog on Earth.

"Wish I could beg like that," Tank said.

"Me, too," Gus said.

None of the other dogs could do it. It was Moon Pie's special gift. Gus often wondered what his own gift was. All the others seemed to have found theirs, but Gus had yet to discover what his was. He spent a lot of time thinking about it.

"Oh, Moonie, you're such an angel, but do watch out so that I don't step on you," Miss Lottie said.

By this time, Moon Pie had edged his foot in close to Miss Lottie's foot, and then, *then*, he drew his own paw back quickly and yipped.

It only took one sharp, pathetic yip.

"Awww, honey, I told you not to get underfoot," Miss Lottie said. She scooped up the small dog and cradled him in her arms. Moon Pie's eyes were larger and sadder than ever now.

"Here," Miss Lottie said, putting him back down. She picked through the fatty slices of roasted pork on the cutting board until she found a piece that seemed right. "I'm sorry, sweetie."

Moon Pie sat back on his haunches and waved one fore-paw in the air. Miss Lottie chuckled as she put the piece of pork in Moon Pie's mouth.

"Oh my Lord, you are so cute," Miss Lottie muttered, shaking her head.

The smell of roasted pork filled the small kitchen. Roo and Tank sniffed the air.

"I can't take it any longer," Tank said. He rose to his feet.

"Me neither!" Roo said.

They surreptitiously wandered over to where the pork was being doled out.

"NO," Miss Lottie said. She gave the two dogs a stern stare. "Tank, you know you're on a diet." She shook her head at him. "Roo, last time I gave you table scraps, you were sick for days. No, this is for Moon Pie." She put another piece in Moon Pie's mouth.

"But you didn't even really step on Moon Pie's toe!" Tank said. "It was all an act!"

Tank often spoke to Miss Lottie, even though he knew she didn't understand. While Miss Lottie was more dog savvy than most, she still only understood about one-third of what they said to her, and she clearly did not understand what Tank was saying now.

Miss Lottie gently pushed Tank aside with her foot. "Come on, old guy, gimme some room here."

Tank grumbled as he shuffled over to his bed and

plopped down onto it. "All I wanted was one piece."

After finishing the pork, Moon Pie tottered over to Tank and curled up on top of his broad back. Tank leaned over and licked a tidbit of pork off Moon Pie's chin.

"That's quite a gift you've got," Roo said.

"Gertie says I can charm the pants off anyone," Moon Pie said. "Gertie says I'll never starve because of it."

Decker, who had been staring out the window, quickly turned his head in Moon Pie's direction. "Who's Gertie?" he asked.

It was the first time Decker had addressed the pack since the dog park. Gus kept quiet. Roo turned to face the wall. Tank shifted his weight and glanced over at Gus.

"Gertie's my human," Moon Pie said. He sat up. "I'm pretty sure she's on vacation with that nasty, nasty sister of hers, but I'm also pretty sure she'll be home soon. And when she brings me back to her house, we'll order french fries at the drive-through and we'll eat sausage on Sundays! And at night we'll eat popcorn and watch TV shows about people behaving badly. Right, Gus, right?"

The only sound in the cramped kitchen was Miss Lottie's knife scraping the cutting board. Moon Pie's ears sat straight up. His tail wagged eagerly.

"Gus . . . ," Tank said.

Gus looked up at the ceiling, hoping something would come to him.

"Gus, he's talking to you! Answer him!" Roo cried.

Gus licked his paw and thought. Moon Pie was so sweet and happy. If Gus told him the truth, that his Gertie had died, he would be sad. Which would make Tank sad, and probably Roo, too.

That wasn't what his pack needed today.

But if he lied now, when would he tell Moon Pie the truth?

"GUS!" Roo said.

Maybe when Moon Pie was older and the pack was settled down a bit.

Yes. That would be the perfect time.

"Gus?" Moon Pie asked. "When do you think I'm going back to Gertie's?"

The sinking feeling swept over him again. Gus ignored it.

"Soon, Moonie," Gus said. "Very soon. She's just on vacation like you said."

Tank and Roo both turned their heads sharply to look at him.

"Right, Tank?" Gus asked. He held his breath and waited for Tank to respond.

Tank paused. He gave his stomach a quick lick. "Right. Gertie will come and get you . . . soon."

"I knew it," Moon Pie said. His voice sounded sleepy and faraway. He eased himself down so that he was sprawled across Tank's back again. Soon he was snoring his soft, sweet snore.

Decker glared at Moon Pie, then stalked out of the room.

"Where's he going?" Tank asked, staring after Decker.

"Probably just looking around," Gus said. "He needs to get used to things."

"If you say so. But I still don't like him. I don't like the way he looks at my Moon Pie."

"I know, Tank, I'll keep an eye on him."

But when Gus felt the hair on his back prickle with alarm, he worried he had made a huge mistake welcoming this dog into the pack.

And lying to Moon Pie. That, too, felt wrong.

Gus got up and nosed around under the sofa until he found an old sock to gnaw on. It wasn't as good as a rock, but it made him feel better about the day's events.

Roo spun in a quick circle. "I don't see what's wrong with the new guy! He seems fine, just fine! At least he can make up his mind!"

Gus sighed. Roo hadn't always been so annoyed with him. In the beginning, she'd clung to Gus. His presence had seemed to calm her down.

Gus had been her friend back then.

Roo Before

On the day of her birth, Roo shot out of her mama—
BAM!

"Ow." Mama winced. Her new puppy was wigglier than the three others had been. She pushed and shoved and pushed her way up to her mama's face and then barked and barked and barked.

Mama licked her forehead. "Hello there! What an eager little thing you are—what's this?" Mama stopped licking. "Well now, that's a first for me. A three-legged pup."

That pup had three *strong* legs, though, and it was soon discovered that she could run faster than any other animal on the farm.

"WATCH MEEEEE!"

She would bark and bark and BARK.

If she got nervous or worried or scared, which was often, she would give herself one big shake and then RUN, with barely a thought as to where she was going.

"GOTTA GOOOOO!"

One day, after a cow mooed especially loudly, the pup ran and ran and ran and ran until . . .

She found herself in a new place. A quieter place. A place without mooing cows.

She sat in front of a man. A new man.

He scooped her up and took her in. He fed her.

It was good for a few days.

"Hey, Tripod, wanna go for a ride?"

That three-legged dog took one look at that loud truck

making *knock-knock-knocking* noises, with its black smoke and its bad smells, and she gave herself a big shake.

"GOTTA GOOOOO!"

She ran and ran and ran and RAN until . . .

She found herself in another new place. With new people.

"HOW DOES THIS KEEP HAPPENING?" She didn't want to keep running, but something deep inside her needed to move, get away, go somewhere new, somewhere safe. Nothing ever felt *right*.

The new people in the new house were good for a while. They fed her and hugged her and gave her fresh water and space to run until . . .

A tiny new human was born. A tiny new human who cried and shrieked and screamed and turned red.

"DON'T LIKE IT, DON'T LIKE IT, DON'T LIKE IT!"

The three-legged dog gave herself one big shake and then she was off and running again, only not quite as fast as before. She ran through alleys, across yards, through forests, over fields. She ran for days, weeks, months.

When she saw the woman, large and solid as a mountain, standing in front of the quiet house next to the quiet dog who was gnawing quietly on a tennis ball, something inside that three-legged dog shifted and clicked into place. This time, *this time*, she felt as though she might be running toward something instead of away from it.

"Hello there," Miss Lottie said. "Perhaps you'd like to join us?"

The three-legged dog let out a long, deep breath.

"Home," she said to the quiet dog.

"Home," he said to her.

Decker

Decker needed to leave the kitchen, where the stupid, spoiled little pug was, before he did something rash.

It was too soon. He knew that.

First he had to investigate this new house. No use putting lots of work into a strategy if the house wasn't right.

The family room bulged with torn chairs and fur-covered sofas. Worn dog beds were tucked into every nook. A metal water bowl had been set in the corner.

For some odd reason, he really liked that metal water bowl.

He could smell dog poop and urine and sweat and socks and hair and lunch meat and soup. All the smells that Decker expected in a house with dogs and an old woman. But there was also a faint smell of something . . . fishy. It was everywhere. In the kitchen. In the family room. He had smelled it before, but he couldn't remember if he had liked it or not.

He poked his head into a tiny bathroom and took it in for a moment. Above the toilet was a child's framed drawing of a dog. Underneath the drawing, the name "Mr. Beans" was written in pencil.

If that's what Miss Lottie thought he looked like, she needed glasses. That dog, with his happy pink tongue and smiling eyes, did not look like Decker at all.

He took a quick sip from the toilet and continued on. A small room on his left caught his attention.

He paused in front of the door and sniffed.

Cat. That was the smell he had been wondering about.

His nose wasn't as good as it once was, but he was sure there was a cat in there somewhere.

He hadn't known many cats in his time. The few he *had* known had never been a problem. He found, actually, that they could be a good source of information.

A sewing machine sat in one corner, surrounded by bags of fabric. In the other corner was a bed. He walked over to it. Sniffed.

"Come out," he said.

Silence.

"I won't hurt you. I just want to ask some questions."

A small white nose poked out from the bottom of the dust ruffle.

36

"Tell me about the pack," Decker said.

The nose retreated back under the bed.

An itchy, prickling hotness spread across Decker's lips and gums. He snapped his mouth open and shut, biting air.

"I *said*, tell me about this pack."

He licked his paw while he waited for a response.

"You should answer when a dog talks to you," he said.

"What are you doing in here?"

Decker turned. Gus had snuck up on him and was standing in the doorway.

"Just talking," Decker said.

"We have an agreement with Ghost," Gus said. "A truce. We don't bother him and he doesn't bother us."

"Interesting."

"It's the way it is," Gus said. He held his head high, but he was still shorter than Decker.

"Who made these rules?" Decker asked.

"We all did."

"Huh," said Decker.

He strode out of the room without giving Gus another look. He continued down the hall to another bedroom.

"Nothing for you in Miss Lottie's room," Gus called after him. "We all sleep in the living room, except . . ."

Decker stopped. He cocked his head to one side and waited for Gus to continue.

"Except what?" Decker asked.

Gus paused.

"Moon Pie sleeps with Miss Lottie. The rest of us sleep in the family room. Moon Pie is new and he's used to sleeping with a human. It's the way it is."

"You keep saying 'it's the way it is,'" Decker said. The burning, itching sensation was growing stronger, more insistent. "I wasn't here when you made these rules."

"The rules work," Gus said.

"Oh? What kind of rules allow the smallest, weakest, youngest member of the pack to sleep with the human?"

Gus growled. "I *allow* Moon Pie to sleep there because he needs humans more than the rest of us. And Miss Lottie has a nightlight so he won't be scared of the dark. It's what's best for him, and what's best for his happiness is best for the pack's happiness. We've all agreed on this rule."

Decker didn't respond. He just strutted into Miss Lottie's bedroom, his head high.

"Suit yourself," Gus said from down the hall.

Decker surveyed the messy bedroom. He immediately went to the wall with the outlet. There was indeed a nightlight in the shape of a dog bone. He sighed.

Good. Very good.

Pictures of Miss Lottie with various dogs were everywhere. On her bureau, on her nightstand.

Decker recognized some of the dogs. The largest frame held a picture of Miss Lottie and Gus. Next to that was a smaller picture frame showing Moon Pie wearing a ridiculous pirate hat. He was in an older woman's lap, and the older woman was looking down at him, laughing. She had one long, white braid that draped across her shoulder and big, round eyeglasses that made her look like a bug.

The infamous Gertie, of course. He studied her closely, from her braid to her glasses, mentally storing the important details.

Roo's picture showed her running across the yard. A picture of Tank highlighted his big belly.

There was a faded picture of a large dog and a young girl. The girl had frizzy hair, and she was smiling at the dog. He took up her entire lap.

Decker moved in closer. The picture of Mr. Beans did look a lot like him. Dark fur. Sharp nose. Pale eyes. Decker studied the way Mr. Beans tilted his head. He noted that the tip of his tongue stuck out the side of his mouth.

Humans were such suckers. All you had to do was tilt your head to one side and stick your tongue out of your mouth and they'd feed you and house you and do whatever you wanted them to.

He knew the moment he met her that Miss Lottie would be easy. Not like some of the other humans he'd known.

A shiver shot through him. He shook it off. No, Miss Lottie was different.

Once she had fallen for his charms, he could begin getting rid of the others. One by one. Starting with the stupid little pug.

When it was finally just him and Miss Lottie, he could

be at peace. There would always be food. He'd never again have to fight for dominance. And with Miss Lottie near him, he would never have to worry about the darkness. If he could just make her love him the most, everything would be perfect.

He looked at the bed. He was pretty sure he could get there in one leap.

He heard footsteps in the hall.

He crouched, ready to spring.

"There you are!" Miss Lottie said. She stood in the doorway with her hands on her hips. "This room is off-limits. If I start letting all you dogs sleep on my bed, I'll never get a moment's rest."

Decker looked at Miss Lottie and saw her warm smile. It was time to see what kind of human she really was.

He tilted his head to one side and let the tip of his tongue stick out.

Miss Lottie clasped her hands to her chest. "Ohh. You're so sweet!" she said.

Decker sprang onto the bed.

Miss Lottie laughed. "Look at you, jumping up there like you own the place." She wagged a finger at him. "Get down, boy. Not enough room here for you and me *and* Moonie."

He lay down on the bed and stared at her, the tip of his tongue poking out of the side of his mouth. When she moved in to pet him, he gently licked her hand.

"What a cutie," Miss Lottie said, shaking her head. "You really are so much like my old Mr. Beans." She laughed and sat down next to him on the bed. "Okay, just for one night. I'm sure Moon Pie won't mind sleeping in the family room this once."

He nestled his head into his forepaws and closed his eyes while she stroked his back.

"Such a good, sweet boy," she murmured.

He had won his first battle with her.

It was an excellent sign.

Moon Pie

Moon Pie did not like sleeping in the family room.
He did not like it one bit.

He always slept in Miss Lottie's bed, and before that he had always slept in Gertie's bed. This was all wrong.

"I don't understand, Gus," Moon Pie said. He was huddled up on his tiny pillow with the dog bone designs on it. "Why can't I sleep in Miss Lottie's bed tonight? Doesn't she like me anymore?"

Gus looked at him from across the room and sighed.

"Moonie, I told you, it has nothing to do with you. Decker is nervous, that's all. He's in a new place. Tomorrow everything will be back to the way it was."

Moon Pie studied Gus. He didn't seem like himself.

Moon Pie was actually not sure he even believed Gus.

"But why can't we both be there?" Moon Pie asked. "Why can't I sleep in the big bed with the new dog *and* Miss Lottie?"

"There's no way you would both fit," Gus said.

"Why?"

Gus growled softly. "Moon Pie, stop. It's just one night. You wouldn't all fit. I don't sleep in Miss Lottie's bed because Miss Lottie's bed is too small for the both of us. The one time I slept there she kicked me in her sleep all night long. The new dog will not like sleeping there and Miss Lottie will not like sleeping with such a big dog, I'm sure of it. And that's that."

"Oh," Moon Pie said. He nestled into his pillow. "Well, I'll be back with Gertie soon, and when I am, I'll always sleep on the big bed, and besides, Gertie's bed is bigger than Miss Lottie's."

He got up and circled once.

"Can I sleep with you, Tank?"

"All right," Tank said gruffly. "But I'm a light sleeper, so don't move around too much."

"I won't!" Moon Pie said. He trotted over to Tank and hopped up on his back.

"Oof," Tank said.

"Now go to sleep, Moonie!" said Roo.

The family room was darker and colder than Miss Lottie's bedroom. And there was a strange ticking noise.

Maybe a clock. Or maybe that spooky-scary cat was clicking his teeth while he was sneaking around doing sneaky things. Did spooky-scary cats click their teeth like that? Moon Pie wasn't sure. He had heard about Ghost, the cat who lived under the bed, but he had never seen him. Seeing Ghost was actually the last thing Moon Pie ever wanted to do.

Soon Moon Pie heard all the other dogs snoring, and he knew he was the only one awake. That's when he heard something else.

Scritch, scritch, scritch.

Moon Pie's ears shot straight up.

Scritch, scritch, scritch.

It was a mouse!

Once, when he was a puppy, a sneaky-pete mouse had skittered across his paws. It almost bit him, too, so he had to race over to Gertie, who had scooped him up and told him everything would be fine, just fine. Then she had kissed him on the top of his head.

Scritch, scritch, scritch.

Moon Pie trembled. Sometimes he heard that sound during the day. Gus said once that it was the shade rubbing against the window. Moon Pie stared into the darkness, but he could only make out lumpy shapes.

Scritch, scritch, scritch.

Moon Pie's heart thumped wildly. That sneaky-pete

mouse was getting closer! Moon Pie got up from Tank's bed carefully, so as not to disturb him.

Swoosh! He raced past the lumpy shapes and scampered into the hall.

Miss Lottie's door stood open. *Hooray!* He sped toward her bedroom and stopped when he got to the doorway.

The familiar sound of Miss Lottie's snoring made him feel calmer. He took two tiny steps into the room, dimly lit by the nightlight.

Something stirred on the bed.

The new dog. Decker. He sat up in the bed and looked down at Moon Pie.

"What are you doing here?" he asked.

"I want up," Moon Pie said softly. "There's a spooky-scary cat and a sneaky-pete mouse and I want UP."

He sat back on his hind legs and waved one paw at Decker.

"Well, well, well," Decker said. "Aren't you something? You want *up.*"

Moon Pie waved the other paw. He made his eyes bigger. He hoped Miss Lottie would wake up and see him.

"Yes," Moon Pie said. "I need to be up on the big bed now, please."

Decker stared down at him. Moon Pie wasn't sure why, but something about the new dog's stare made him more afraid than the sneaky-pete mouse and the spooky-scary

cat put together. He wanted to run away, but his need to be up was stronger.

"Do you always get what you want?" Decker asked.

Moon Pie wasn't sure how to answer that. He actually did get whatever he wanted, almost always, but he kept his mouth shut.

"You can tell me," Decker said. "It's okay. Do you always get what you want?"

It still sounded like a trick question.

"Sometimes," Moon Pie said. "But not always."

"Ah."

"Can you wake Miss Lottie so I can come up now?"

"Moon Pie, what do you think is the most important thing a dog can learn in a pack?"

Moon Pie sat. This new dog had such odd questions and comments. He didn't understand him at all.

"Ummm, is it 'the pack comes first'?" Moon Pie asked.

"No," Decker said calmly. "That's not right. Think harder."

Moon Pie scrunched his eyebrows together. The new dog was trying to teach him something. Gus did that all the time. He tried hard to think of the right answer. He liked it when Gus quizzed him and he got the right answer.

"Ummm, is it 'stay away from skunks'?" he asked.

"No, Moon Pie, it's not."

"Oh."

"Would you like to know what it is, then?"

Moon Pie wasn't quite sure. But maybe if he said yes, the new dog would wake up Miss Lottie and he could get up on the big bed.

"Yes," Moon Pie said. He put his front paws against the side of the bed.

"The most important thing about the pack is that you know your place in it. And you, Moon Pie, are the weakest, smallest, silliest member of the pack."

"I am?"

"Yes, Moon Pie. You are the lowest member. Lower than the cat."

"But . . . but . . . no one else has told me that . . ."

"Things are changing around here. I am the top dog now. I'm the one who sleeps on the big bed. You do not. You are the lowest of the low."

He looked calmly at Moon Pie.

"Understand?"

"But, but—"

"Quiet! What I say goes."

Moon Pie started to whimper.

"You're not a puppy anymore. Stop sniveling."

"I can't help it!" Moon Pie said. "I don't like sleeping in the family room! There are mice and cats and—"

"You'll soon learn that you can't get everything you want just because you're small and *cute*."

The way Decker said "cute" made Moon Pie quiver. His heart was beating too fast. Everything felt very, very wrong.

The new dog snarled.

"I said—"

"MOON PIE! Come here!"

Moon Pie spun around.

Tank stood in the doorway with his chest puffed out. He growled.

Miss Lottie mumbled something in her sleep. Moon Pie hesitated. If he could just get back on the bed, maybe everything would be better—

"Get over here now, Moonie!" Tank said.

Moon Pie knew when Tank was mad. He trotted out of the bedroom. As he was leaving, he heard the new dog grumble.

"Worthless little mutt."

Tank

Tank felt the tips of his ears growing hotter as he stormed away from Miss Lottie's bedroom with Moon Pie at his heels.

"What were you doing in there?" Tank asked gruffly.

Moon Pie scurried to keep up with him. "It was so dark in the family room, and there was a weird scratchy noise, and I thought it might be a sneaky-pete mouse, or a spooky-scary cat, or—"

Tank stopped walking. Moon Pie, who was slightly out of breath, stopped next to him.

"Moonie, you know I'll always protect you, right?"

Moon Pie paused. "I guess," he said quietly.

"You guess? Haven't I been there for you since the very first day you arrived?"

Moon Pie tilted his head to one side. "Yeah," he said. His tail wagged twice. "You have."

"All right, then! I'm certainly not going to stop now! You have nothing to worry about, Moonie. I'm here for you." He nudged Moon Pie's side with his nose. "Come on. I'm tired and I'm sure you are, too." He continued into the family room and plopped down on his bed. Soon he felt Moon Pie curling up next to him.

"Good night, Moonie."

"Night, Tank."

Seconds later, Tank could hear Moon Pie's soft snores. Tank turned from side to side, but he couldn't get comfortable. So many angry thoughts raced through his mind.

Decker had threatened Moon Pie. *His* Moon Pie! Tank couldn't believe anyone could be such a bully to sweet little Moonie. What would make this new dog behave like that?

Tank had hated bullies ever since he was a puppy. He had been the largest in the litter, and his mother had told him it was his responsibility to take care of his smaller siblings.

"It's the right thing to do," she always said.

Tank had taken his job seriously. He kept his brothers and sisters safe from the vacuum cleaner. He helped them down slippery stairs. He chased bad neighborhood dogs away from the fence in the yard.

This new dog would never do those things. It was

obvious he didn't care about anyone but himself. He was just a big, selfish bully.

Tank would have to speak to Gus about Decker tomorrow. Something needed to be done quickly before Decker hurt Moon Pie.

Tank Before

Tank found his dog gift early in life.

"You are a guardian, Tank," his mother often told him. "It's your gift. You do it better than dogs twice your size."

Tank knew it was true. He felt it in every bone in his body. And so when he was adopted by a family with two chubby, grabby twin boys, he protected them with the same fierce loyalty with which he had once protected his siblings.

When one of them crawled too close to the edges of the glass coffee table, Tank stood between the twin and the table so the twin couldn't bump against its edges and cut himself.

When strangers came to the door, Tank barked and snarled until he was sure they meant no harm.

When the new kitten got on top of the refrigerator and could not get down, Tank dragged his bed over for her to jump onto and barked until she did it.

He was everyone's bodyguard, and he loved his job.

When the accident happened, Tank was sleeping on the sofa. The twins had just learned to walk, and sometimes they fell. This kept Tank on guard most of the time, but at that crucial moment he was taking a well-deserved nap.

Tank woke up in time to see one twin push the other against the glass coffee table. The cut was deep. The hurt twin looked stunned. Tank hopped down from the sofa to help.

Blood poured down the toddler's face. Tank wanted to help, *needed* to help. He barked and got on top of the boy, who was rolling back and forth on the floor. If he could just keep the boy still, maybe he would calm down. Then Tank could lick the boy's face like his mother had when he got hurt as a pup.

The boy started to whimper, then burst into a howl of pain.

The other twin crawled over, waving the TV remote at his brother. The remote had sharp edges, and the boy was clumsy. Tank growled at the boy, hoping that would scare him away.

And that was when the parents came in. They screamed louder than the twin.

It took Tank a moment to realize that they were screaming at him.

"Tank, OFF!" cried the mother. She shoved him off the boy. "Where were you?" she asked the twins' father angrily.

"I just went to the bathroom for a second—hey, don't be so rough!"

"He's on top of our son and he's growling! Get him out of here!"

"But—"

"NOW."

The father pulled Tank out to the yard by his collar. Tank stayed there for a long, long time, worrying about his twins, wondering if they were okay.

Later that day, the father drove Tank to a small building with small windows. Inside it smelled of fear and mange. Tank heard the wails and whines of other dogs.

The father brought Tank up to the desk and handed his leash to the woman there.

"We can't keep this dog any longer," he said.

The woman behind the desk got up quickly.

"Sir, we need you to fill out some forms—"

"I can't," the father said. "I just can't."

He walked away without looking back.

A woman was nearby. A woman with gray, frizzy hair. She bent down and held Tank's head in her hands.

"I'll take him," she said.

"Now, Lottie," said the woman behind the desk. "You don't know anything about this dog."

"I've been volunteering here a long time," Miss Lottie said, "and I know a good dog when I see one. This guy looks like he might make a good guard dog, too."

A good guard dog. That's what Tank had always thought he was. But ever since that day, he hadn't been sure.

Gus

T he family room was still dark. Gus could hear Tank and Roo snoring. He smelled Moon Pie's deep sleep. Moon Pie had been awake earlier in the night and had wandered off, but Tank, his ever-vigilant guardian, had brought him back. Moon Pie settled in right away. After tossing and turning for a while, Tank finally fell asleep. Gus lifted his head and sniffed the air.

Ghost was nearby.

Ghost had been adopted just a few days after Gus. At first Ghost had stayed under the bed. Gus desperately wanted an animal friend, someone who understood how long and lonely the days could be when Miss Lottie left the house to run errands. Day after day he would call out to Ghost, pleading with him to come out and talk, but the cat kept quiet.

Then one night, Gus woke up with a start and found Ghost batting a paper clip across the family room floor. Gus watched him for a while, trying to figure out the best way to approach the shy cat. The more he watched, the more he realized Ghost was showing off. For him. Gus finally understood what to do. He had simply said, "You're good at that."

"I know," was all Ghost said back.

Ever since that night, the two had forged a tenuous friendship. Ghost would sometimes come into the family room to complain about the toys Miss Lottie was always giving him, which lacked catnip and were therefore inferior.

Other times Gus would go to the guest room and quietly talk about whatever was on his mind—his pack, his food, rocks. Gus always felt that Ghost was truly listening to him in a focused, catlike way.

What fascinated Gus most about Ghost was that he was such a *cat*. As much as Gus hated to admit it, Ghost was smarter and more observant than any dog he had ever spoken to. Gus was sure Ghost had definite ideas about the new dog, and he wanted to hear them.

Once Gus's eyes adjusted to the dark, he could see the outlines of the slim white cat sitting on top of the bookshelves. Gus trotted over and sat down in front of them.

"I've been hearing a mouse," he said.

"Old news," Ghost said. He lifted up his paw and started grooming. "I've known about him for ages. I like keeping him around, though. It's fun."

"I suppose," Gus said, although he didn't really understand the mouse thing. He was more of a squirrel guy.

"So what do you think of Decker?" Gus asked.

Ghost stopped licking his paw for a moment. He turned to stare at Gus. Sometimes, when those big, owl eyes shone on Gus, he felt a strange quiver tunnel its way through his body. His mouth would twitch, and he found himself yearning to bite Ghost very, very badly. He didn't want to do it, but he could feel his doggy instinct swelling up inside him. He prided himself on being able to keep this urge checked.

"I find him . . . disturbing," Ghost said.

"Really? How?"

Ghost lifted his other paw and started licking it. "For one thing, he threatened me."

"That's not so strange," Gus said. "Dogs threaten cats all the time."

"This was different. Can't explain it," Ghost said. "Something about his tone."

That, Gus understood. The aloofness and arrogance of the new dog made Gus uneasy, too.

"Didn't like the way he talked to Moon Pie, either," Ghost said. "Not that I was eavesdropping."

"Of course not."

"He wasn't very pleasant. Granted, Moon Pie is a terrible nuisance, but this seemed a bit . . . harsh." Ghost swatted a pen off the shelf.

"Can you keep an eye on Decker?" Gus asked. "I wouldn't want you to eavesdrop. I know it's beneath you. But maybe, if you happen to hear something interesting, you could report back to me."

Ghost tilted his head slightly. One ear twitched. "Why should I do that?"

Gus thought for a moment. "How about I bring you a Tiddle Widdle Chicken Bit every morning?"

Ghost swished his tail.

"Two."

Miss Lottie only gave out two Tiddle Widdle Chicken Bits a day to each dog. If he gave both to Ghost, he wouldn't have any.

Gus thumped his tail once.

"Deal," he said.

His pack was worth a thousand Tiddle Widdle Chicken Bits.

Before he fell asleep, he thought about what Ghost had said. A conversation between Decker and Moon Pie was troublesome. The young pug was so easily influenced. Gus would have to pay extra attention to Decker when Moon Pie was around.

Moon Pie Before

The first face Moon Pie saw every morning was Gertie's, and the first face Gertie saw was Moon Pie's.

They had their breakfast together, and then they napped. They watched TV, had a little bitty something for lunch, and then they napped. They ate their dinner, watched more TV, and napped some more.

They did go for walks, but not for long walks, oh no. Moon Pie liked to be up on the big bed, and Gertie did, too.

Some days, when Gertie got the sniffles, they stayed in bed all day watching TV and eating popcorn. These were Moon Pie's favorite days. And when Gertie stayed in bed for days and days and days, Moon Pie was happiest of all, since it meant lots of popcorn.

When Gertie had the sniffles, a lady with gray, frizzy

hair named Miss Lottie came by. She would walk Moon Pie up and down the block and then bring him back to the big bed. Then she and Gertie would talk about Gertie's "treasure."

"You'll be in charge of my little treasure when the time comes, won't you, Lottie?" Gertie asked often.

"I most definitely will, Gertie. You can count on me."

Moon Pie knew what the treasure was, of course. It was popcorn. Gertie was worried about her popcorn and wanted to be sure Miss Lottie knew where it was in case anything happened, like a flood or a fire or something. Popcorn was very important, and Moon Pie was glad Gertie told Miss Lottie all about it.

One day Gertie's nasty, nasty sister came to the house. She fussed over all the popcorn kernels and the dog hair on Gertie's bed. She locked Moon Pie up in his kennel in the basement, which he hadn't used since he was a tiny puppy.

He stayed there for what seemed like forever until Miss Lottie came to take him on his walk. Only this time, they walked a new way.

"You'll like it at my house," Miss Lottie said. She seemed to have caught Gertie's sniffles, because she wiped her nose with a handkerchief. "But first we'll go to the park and meet the rest of the pack."

Moon Pie liked the other dogs right away, and they liked him. Roo played chase. Tank played tug with the rope. Gus licked the top of his head and told him he was a good boy.

Later, when they were at Miss Lottie's house, Moon Pie smelled a familiar smell.

Popcorn! Miss Lottie made it just for him!

Miss Lottie took him to her big bed and they ate popcorn and watched TV.

And while Miss Lottie's bed wasn't quite as big as Gertie's, her popcorn was even better. And she gave Moon Pie *salami*. Moon Pie loved salami.

It was just about the best day ever.

Gus

Even though it was a quiet Saturday morning, Gus nervously gnawed on a rock in Miss Lottie's small yard as he watched the other dogs do their business. He wondered, briefly, if chewing on things that were not food was his special dog gift. He was very good at it, better than any other dog he had ever met. Still, it wasn't a very useful talent.

He kept a careful eye on Decker, who had sauntered off into the corner. There was a thick patch of fir trees and bushes there that none of the other dogs ventured into. The low, full bushes scratched the dogs' sides, so they had learned to stay in the open spaces.

Gus thought about his conversation with Ghost the night before. If what Ghost had said was true, Gus would have to speak to Decker about it.

He hated confrontation, especially with a new dog. He shifted the rock to the other side of his mouth and chewed.

Roo wandered across the grass, nose down, looking for the right spot to pee. Moon Pie inspected a dying rosebush.

Tank sat next to Gus. "What's the new guy doing?" he asked.

"Just investigating," Gus said.

"Sure," Tank said.

Moon Pie plunked down next to Gus. "Am I the lowest member of the pack?" he asked.

"Where did you get that idea?" Gus asked sharply. The question made his neck hairs tingle. He would never, ever imply that any of his pack members were "lower" than the others.

"I don't know," Moon Pie said. He glanced at the corner of the yard.

"I bet I know exactly how he got that idea in his head," Tank growled.

Just then, Decker strode out from behind a fir. He stopped when he saw Tank.

"What's your problem?" Decker asked.

"YOU," Tank said. "Why are you telling Moon Pie he's the lowest member of the pack?"

"I don't know what you're talking about," Decker said. He lay down on the grass and closed his eyes.

Tank waddled over. He stood above Decker and barked.

Decker raised his head. "What?"

"Don't ever talk to my Moon Pie again about ANY-THING, do you hear me?"

Decker growled. "I'll talk to him whenever I feel like it."

"NO, YOU WON'T!" Tank yelled.

Tank's barking grew louder. Roo howled.

Gus heard the back door open.

"Everybody, BE QUIET!" Miss Lottie yelled.

Tank stopped barking. Roo, who hated being scolded, scampered under the deck to hide.

"That's better," Miss Lottie said. She went back into the house.

Decker got to his feet.

"Get out of my way," he said.

"No," Tank said. He leaned in toward Decker. The fur stood up along his back, and he looked Decker right in the eyes and growled.

"I dare you to take a step closer," Decker said.

"Tank, stay where you are!" Gus said.

"WATCH OUT!" Roo said from under the deck.

Tank took a step closer.

Decker sat on his haunches, glaring at Tank. The two dogs were almost nose to nose.

Gus's heart quickened. He took a step toward them, but then paused. Sometimes dogs needed to work things out themselves, without the pack leader stepping in.

Moon Pie whimpered. "Don't let them fight!" he said.

"Gus, MAKE THEM STOP!" Roo said.

But there were also times when those fights went too far and dogs got hurt.

He stared at the two dogs, his body quivering. Should he, or shouldn't he?

Then Decker did something so odd, so startlingly strange, that for a moment Gus didn't understand what was happening.

Decker brought his own paw up to his mouth and bit it. Hard.

"What—" Tank began.

Decker continued biting his paw until it started to bleed. Then he lifted his head to the sky and yelped.

"*What are you doing?*" Tank asked again. His tail was tense, his legs rooted to the ground.

Decker pinned his ears back and yelped again.

Gus barked once—a high, startled yip. When he heard the back door slam, he whipped his head around and saw Miss Lottie running across the grass.

"Oh my goodness, what's happened?" she yelled.

As soon as Decker saw she was watching him, he shrieked again and tucked his tail between his legs. He kept his eyes on Tank as he skittered sideways over to the edge of the yard.

"Tank, what did you do?" Miss Lottie asked. Her frown was deep as she hurried over to Decker.

"What happened?"

Quinn stood by the back gate, eyes wide. He had his hand on the latch but wasn't pushing it open.

"Tank bit Decker!" Miss Lottie said.

"What?"

Miss Lottie nodded. She crouched next to Decker, who was whimpering by the fence. "I'll take Tank inside and lock him in his kennel. Then I'll drive Decker to the vet. Can you give the dogs their breakfast and medicine while I'm gone?"

"Okay," Quinn said. He stared at Tank, shaking his head. "But that's not like Tank. He would never bite."

"Well, he must have snapped for some reason," Miss Lottie said. She was out of breath and wiping sweat from her forehead. "All I know is that Decker here probably needs stitches."

She gently picked up Decker's paw. The paw he'd bitten himself. He yelped when she held it a certain way.

"Okay, buddy, I'll get you to the vet. First let me take Tank here to his kennel."

She walked slowly over to Tank, like he was a bomb waiting to go off. "Come here, Tank. That's a good boy."

Tank was still standing in the middle of the yard, looking confused.

"Here, boy, here, Tank," Miss Lottie said. She slowly reached down and held Tank's collar. "Let's go in, okay?"

"Gus, I didn't do it! I swear!" Tank said as Miss Lottie led him into the house.

"I know, Tank, I know!" Gus said.

But knowing Tank was innocent didn't help. Miss Lottie thought he was guilty, and that was all that mattered.

Quinn

Quinn peered under the deck. He could see Roo huddled in the far corner.

"Come on out, Roo," he said softly. "Come on, girl, it's fine."

Roo stayed where she was. Quinn understood wanting to hide. Sometimes, when his mom was gone for the day, Quinn would wedge a chair up against his bedroom door. Jessie and his friends could say whatever they wanted to from the other side, but at least they couldn't poke. They couldn't shove. They couldn't trip.

His phone rang. He ignored it. That was their newest form of taunting. Call, then hang up as soon as Quinn answered.

"Come on, you two, let's go inside." Patting his leg,

Quinn beckoned to Moon Pie and Gus. They followed him into the house.

When Quinn opened the back door, he was immediately hit by the warm, furry smell of dogs. It was a comforting smell. To Quinn, that smell meant safety. Safety from Jessie and his friends.

Quinn poured kibble into Gus's and Moon Pie's bowls. He tore off pieces of hot dog buns, smushed their vitamins and pills inside, and then sprinkled the bits of bread on top of the kibble.

He held the bowls above their heads, waiting for them to do their silly food dance. But they didn't move.

"Huh. You don't seem very excited about your breakfast," Quinn said, placing the bowls down on the kitchen floor.

They usually dug in frantically when their food was placed before them, but today they sniffed and picked at it.

"Come on, you've got to eat," Quinn said.

Both dogs looked up at him, their eyes questioning.

Quinn sighed. "I don't think Tank did it, if that's what you're wondering," he said. He gave them both a pat on the head. "Eat your breakfast, okay?"

They bent down and started crunching on their food, looking up at Quinn every once in a while for reassurance.

Roo scratched at the back door.

"Come on in, girl," Quinn said. He opened the door

for her and watched as she crept in, head low.

"It'll be okay, I promise," he said. He prepared her breakfast and placed it in front of her. She ate with the same hesitancy that Gus and Moon Pie had showed.

Quinn prepared Tank's food, medicine, and vitamins and carried his bowl into the laundry room where the kennels were. Miss Lottie sometimes put the dogs there after a fight. Quarrels were rare. Usually it was just Roo growling or barking at one of the other dogs. Roo was easily upset.

Tank was curled up in his crate with his back pushed against the wire door.

Quinn's stomach clenched when he saw how forlorn Tank was. Maybe some kibble would help. Tank loved his kibble.

"Breakfast time," Quinn said.

Tank lifted his head, but that was all.

Quinn crouched down and opened Tank's kennel.

"Come on out, Tank," he said. "I put a little extra food in your bowl."

Tank didn't move.

"Come on, boy. I know you didn't do it. There's no way. Miss Lottie must be wrong."

Tank shifted.

"You've got to eat, Tank. Please?" Quinn tried to keep his voice from trembling, but it was hard. Tank—lovable, huggable Tank. Quinn hated seeing the big guy like this.

Tank turned around in his kennel so that he was facing out. His huge head hung down low.

"There you are," Quinn said. He reached in and stroked Tank's rough coat. "Come on out, boy."

The door hung open. But instead of coming out, Tank plopped down again with an *oof.*

"Oh, Tank," Quinn said. He gently rubbed the sides of Tank's face. "Don't worry. I'll convince Miss Lottie that she's wrong about this."

Quinn had no idea how he'd do that, but he was going to try.

His phone rang again. He sighed and clicked it off.

Some days he felt so tired and alone. Today was one of those days.

Quinn Before

There once was a time when Quinn and his older brother played together. He and Jessie threw rocks at cans and built forts in the woods. They took their dog, Murph, on long walks, taking turns holding the leash.

But then Quinn's dad died. He fell over while cutting the grass and never got up again. The doctors said his heart had simply stopped.

Only four days later, when Quinn and Jessie were out for a walk, Murph got off the leash and was hit by a car. He died right in front of them.

It was over in seconds. Quinn wasn't even sure what really happened.

"Why did you let go of the leash?" Jessie asked him, day after day after day.

"I thought you had it!" Quinn said each time.

Pretty soon after that, Jessie stopped playing with Quinn. Then he stopped talking to him.

Quinn began to wonder if maybe it *was* his fault that Murph had died. Had he let go of the leash? He went over and over it but was never really sure.

Four months later, Quinn's mom moved them to a new town and a new house.

"For a fresh start," she said.

They moved in August, and at first everything seemed okay. Packing up the stuff in his old room had helped Quinn take his mind off his dad and Murph. His new room had a window that looked out onto a big tree. The thick branches were perfect for a tree house. He even sketched plans for it. He hoped that maybe Jessie would start talking to him again, and that they could build it together some day.

Things were beginning to feel a little better, day by day.

But then, at their new school, Jessie started hanging out with Cole and Sam. When the three of them got together, things happened.

It started out small. Mumbled insults. Shoves in the hallway. They would wait for Quinn at school, in the park, in the boys' bathroom. The shoves turned to quick punches and sly kicks to the shins. Jessie didn't do it, but he didn't stop it, either. He just watched.

With a target on his back, Quinn had trouble making friends.

At home, he and Jessie would sit in silence in front

of the TV until it was time for dinner.

In some ways, their life went on just like it had before. Mom paid the bills, cooked the meals, went to work, cleaned the house. She was trying, Quinn knew, to keep things running smoothly. To keep things under control. But they had gradually stopped talking about Dad and Murph, as if their memories were like the old photo albums they had tucked away in the basement of the new house.

What Quinn wanted to do more than anything, though, was talk about them. He worried that if he didn't, his memories of them would fade away.

"Didn't Dad like pot roast?" Quinn asked one night at dinner. The question popped out of his mouth before he had a chance to think about it. They were having pot roast, and for some reason it reminded him of Dad.

Mom sighed.

"Yes," she said simply. But that was it, and they never had pot roast again.

After a few more tries, Quinn gave up trying to talk about Dad, Murph, or even their old house. He locked away everything he knew about Life Before in a special place in his brain, like a bureau with a secret drawer. Occasionally, when he was by himself, he'd open that drawer, but mostly he kept it locked.

The taunting texts from Jessie's friends started the second week of school. Then they flooded in daily. Even hourly. He wanted to stop reading them, but for some reason he couldn't. He read every one. Texts about his clothes. His hair. His voice.

One day, while watching TV with Jessie, Quinn blurted out a question that had bothered him for weeks.

"Why don't you ask Cole and Sam to stop texting me?"

It felt like a fair question. Jessie was their friend. He could make it all stop if he wanted to.

"What's the big deal? They're only texts," Jessie said.

Quinn stared at his brother for a moment. "Only" texts? Without a word, he went straight to his room to tear up the drawings of the tree house. It would never happen. Not with Jessie.

Then, on the first day of October, a flier appeared on a tree in front of Quinn's house.

WANTED: ANIMAL LOVER WHO CAN HELP OUT BEFORE AND AFTER SCHOOL WITH MY SECONDHAND DOGS.

There was a phone number and a group picture of the dogs. It was the picture that caught his attention. A three-legged dog. An old bulldog with a round belly. And a shaggy dog standing in the middle.

Quinn stepped in closer to get a better look at the shaggy dog. The dog's eyes were partially covered with scruff, but

Quinn could still see his expression. He looked uncertain, as though he were sitting on a pile of blocks that could be knocked down at any moment. Quinn knew how that felt.

Quinn wasn't sure about many things in his life, but he was sure this was the right job for him.

Miss Lottie only had one question when she met Quinn. "How soon can you start?"

Gus

Gus went back to the laundry room. He had visited Tank three times that day. Each time, Tank had been asleep, his snores filling the small room.

Gus had replayed the incident in his mind over and over, and he always came to the same conclusion—it was all his fault. He should have stopped Decker. He should have stepped between him and Tank. Instead, he had just sat there and done nothing. It was his job to keep the peace, and he had failed.

Gus wished again, for the millionth time, that his special dog gift was being a good leader. If it was, this never would have happened.

Quinn had tried to get Tank to eat earlier, but it was no use. Tank wouldn't leave his kennel. Now it was late afternoon and time for dinner, yet Tank still didn't seem to care.

"Tank?"

No response.

"Tank?" Gus asked again. "You okay?"

Tank opened one eye. "What do you think?" he said.

"It's not that big a deal, Tank. Miss Lottie will get over it."

"She thinks I bit him. She thinks I'm a *biter*." He turned in his crate so that his back was to Gus.

Gus sighed. Miss Lottie did seem mad at Tank. When she came home from the vet, she had gone straight to her bedroom with Decker. She hadn't even stopped to see how Tank was doing.

"She'll forgive you," Gus said. "She's the forgiving type."

Gus couldn't see Tank's face, but he saw his ears twitch for a moment. Tank raised his head, but he didn't turn to face Gus.

"I would never, ever bite. How could she think I bit him? *How*?"

"I don't know," Gus said. "This new dog—"

"I told you not to let him in, Gus. I told you. But you didn't listen to me."

"Tank, I—"

Just then, Quinn entered the laundry room. He picked up the old food and dumped it into the garbage.

"Hey, Gus," Quinn said. He put a fresh bowl of food

down for Tank and opened his kennel door. "Your food is in the kitchen."

Gus stayed where he was.

"Okay." Quinn knelt down and rubbed Gus behind the ears. "Just don't eat Tank's food."

Gus was often amazed at how well Quinn understood dogs. He was even better than Miss Lottie when it came to reading the pack's mood.

"Come on out, Tank," Quinn said. He crouched down next to his kennel. "I put a treat in your bowl."

Tank got up and turned toward his bowl.

"I don't feel like eating," Tank said to Gus.

"Maybe it will help you feel better," Gus said.

"That's not what I need." Tank lay down on the floor of his kennel.

"Oh, Tank," Quinn said. He shook the bowl of food. When Tank didn't budge, Quinn gave him one more pat on the head, then left.

"Maybe he'll be able to convince Miss Lottie that she's wrong," Gus said.

"Maybe he won't be able to," Tank said.

The image of Decker biting his own paw—*his own paw*—swooshed into Gus's thoughts for a moment.

Decker was bad. It was as simple as that. And something needed to be done about it.

"I'll make this right, Tank. I promise."

Quinn

It **was late. but Quinn** didn't care. He knew Miss Lottie needed him, so he helped out more than usual. As he cleaned up the drool and the stray bits of kibble from the dogs' dinners, he thought of Tank. He tried to imagine the gentle giant biting the new dog. He could picture Tank barking and puffing out his chest, but that was it.

Miss Lottie finally came out of her bedroom just as the sun was setting. Her gray hair was more messed up than usual. She gave him a tired smile.

"Thanks for staying late, Quinn," Miss Lottie said. She sank down into a chair at the kitchen table. "You're a good kid."

Quinn got out a jar of peanut butter. He scooped a dollop onto a spoon, pushed Roo's pill into it, and then held the spoon out to her.

"Here you go," Quinn said.

Roo ignored it.

"Roo, come on, now," Miss Lottie said. "Take your medicine."

Roo did one quick circle on her bed.

"Roo, you love peanut butter," Quinn said. She didn't like the hot dog buns for her pills the way the others did. She only ate her pills with peanut butter.

"Come on, Roo, please?" he asked.

She tilted her head, then licked the peanut butter off the spoon.

"Good girl!" He patted her on the back. "She's been nervous all day. They all have."

Miss Lottie put her elbows on the table and cradled her head in her hands. "It's been a long day for everyone."

"I hope they calm down soon."

"Me, too," Miss Lottie said. "I think it's best if Decker sleeps with me again tonight. He's curled up on my bed now. He's still drowsy from the stitches."

Quinn picked up Gus's eye drops. He bent down next to Gus and gently squeezed one into each eye. Gus blinked, stretched, then walked back to his bed.

"Oh, hey, remind me to get new tags for Moon Pie. He's still wearing the ones Gertie gave him," Miss Lottie said. "Can't believe it's only been a month. Seems like we've had that little angel forever."

Quinn frowned as he screwed the cap back on the eye

drops. "Do you really think Tank bit Decker? It doesn't seem like Tank, you know?"

Miss Lottie waved her hand dismissively. "These spats always happen when a new dog arrives. They'll work things out. Anyway, let's hope Tank learns his lesson."

Moon Pie, who had been napping on his bed, sat up and whimpered.

"Aw, Moon Pie, are you still hungry?" Miss Lottie asked. "Maybe you want some popcorn?"

Instead of jumping up, Moon Pie turned around to face the wall.

Quinn shook his head. "He misses Tank. They all do."

"Maybe," Miss Lottie said.

"Can I bring Tank out now?" Quinn asked. "I know he's sorry."

Miss Lottie paused.

"Decker is in your bedroom and you said yourself he's not budging. Tank gets along with everyone else."

"Okay," she said finally. "He can't stay in there forever. I'm sure he's cooled off by now."

Quinn was already in the laundry room by the time Miss Lottie finished her sentence. He bent down and peered into the kennel. Tank was facing away from him.

"You can come out!" Quinn said, opening the kennel door. "Everyone wants to see you."

Tank's ears were up, but he didn't turn around.

"Come on, boy," Quinn said, a waver in his voice. "Come out."

He saw Tank's chest heave a long, heavy sigh.

"All right, maybe you just need to hang out in here for a while."

That night, Quinn walked his bike home instead of riding it to give himself time to think. When he'd asked Miss Lottie if she had seen Tank bite Decker, she said no. So if she hadn't actually seen it happen, it wasn't a sure thing. Maybe the new dog had started it by growling at Moon Pie. There was no way Tank would sit by while another dog picked on the little pug.

Quinn couldn't help but think that Miss Lottie had it wrong. It was way too coincidental that things had gotten out of hand right after this new dog arrived.

He knew strange things went on that grown-ups didn't know about, and he was pretty sure Miss Lottie just wasn't seeing what was really happening.

Decker

Decker whimpered.

Something was on him.

Something bad.

He couldn't breathe. He tried to bark, but no sound came out.

When the pain finally woke him, Decker found himself wrapped up in sheets. He had been dreaming again of the dark place. He lay panting, too afraid to look around.

Too dark too dark TOO DARK.

He started to tremble, his whole body a jumble of quivering nerves, then—

"Hrmph."

Miss Lottie turned on her side.

He sighed, relieved. While he couldn't say he loved Miss

Lottie, or even liked her, she did make him feel safe. He shook his head and breathed in her toothpaste snores.

He was okay. It was only another nightmare.

His paw throbbed. He inhaled Miss Lottie's sleepy smell and put his head back on the pillow. The pain was good. It made dogs strong, and Decker, who had been through a lot in his life, was stronger than most. The pain fed him, kept him alert, kept him fierce. And it kept the darkness away for a while.

A dry, salty taste filled his mouth. He needed water. He looked to the doorway and saw a dim glow coming from the kitchen. But it was still so dark. Would there be enough light for him to find his way?

He hopped off the bed and slowly, carefully made his way down the dark hall, his heart beating wildly.

Something was coming toward him. He could detect movement and a small shape in the dim light.

His fur tingled. His breaths came in faster.

What was it?

He slowly backed away, hoping and praying it didn't sense his fear.

"Who's there?" he demanded.

"Oh, hi," came a small voice.

It was just the stinking little pug, nothing more. Decker gave himself a shake. He had been thinking a lot about Moon Pie. Planning. He had seen the way the pack looked when Moon Pie brought up Gertie. She was dead, obviously. Gus, being weak, didn't know how to tell Moon Pie.

It was all very useful.

And now here was Moon Pie, hopping down the hallway like a stupid rabbit.

"What are you doing up?" Decker asked.

"I, um . . . ," Moon Pie said.

"You're not *scared* again, are you?"

"No, I'm not, not really."

But Moon Pie's big eyes said otherwise. Decker could almost feel the small dog's fluttery heartbeat. His own heart still beat quickly. He willed it to slow down.

Decker sat down and stared for a few moments. "Do they sometimes call you 'Moonie'?"

"Y-yes, sometimes," Moon Pie said.

"What is it that you want, *Moonie*?"

"I was sort of hoping that Miss Lottie might let me up on the big bed? It's really dark in the family room."

"Moonie, I'm sorry," Decker said. "I can't let you up on the big bed. It's just not right."

"Because I'm the lowest member of the pack?"

"Yes."

"Oh."

"But you know, I bet your human, Gertie, would let you up on the big bed!" Decker said. He got to his feet and wagged his tail. "I bet she misses you! Don't you think?"

"Well, yes, but Gertie is still at her nasty, nasty sister's house," Moon Pie said. "She's not home."

"But that's not true." Decker cocked his head to one side. He hoped he looked concerned. He was not actually sure what concern looked like, but he hoped he at least managed to fake it well. "When I was in the shelter, a woman came by asking about a small pug."

Moon Pie's tail wagged once. "What?"

"Yes, yes," Decker said. "She had a long white braid and big eyeglasses." He considered saying how they made her look like a bug, but thought better of it. "She had something in her hand, too," Decker said. "Could it have been"—he looked up at the ceiling—"a pirate hat?"

"YES!" Moon Pie said. "Gertie had a long white braid and glasses and she liked to put me in hats! She loved that pirate hat on me!"

"Oh, well, she's looking for you!"

"Really?" Moon Pie said. His tail wagged rapidly. "I thought she was still on vacation with her nasty, nasty sister! No one told me she was back!"

"I bet she misses you quite a bit."

"You think so?" Moon Pie asked. He paused and tilted his head to one side. "But I don't understand. Why did Miss Lottie take me, then, if Gertie wasn't really gone on vacation?"

Decker stared hard at Moon Pie. "I don't think you want to know why," he said.

"Oh," Moon Pie said. "But—"

"Never mind about that, Moonie!" Decker said. He nudged Moon Pie with his nose. "I think Gertie is probably very worried about you. Otherwise, why would she be looking for you at the shelter? You don't want her to be worried, do you?"

"No!" Moon Pie said. "Not at all!"

"Well then, you should be a good dog and go to her."

"Yes, yes, I should!" Moon Pie let out a small yip. He spun in a quick circle, then stopped. "But how?"

"Oh, that's easy," Decker said. "You know that patch of trees in the back of the yard?"

"Yes," Moon Pie said. "But no one ever goes there."

"Well, I did," Decker said. "And I found something very, very interesting. There's a hole in the fence. You could fit through it easily!"

"Really?" Moon Pie's brow furrowed. "You think?"

"I know it," Decker said.

"You think I could go tomorrow?" Moon Pie asked. His big eyes widened and his tail was still wagging furiously.

"I don't see why not. Just sneak out there when no one is looking."

"Oh," Moon Pie said. His tail went limp. "I was sort of hoping that Gus or Tank could come with me."

"No, Moonie. You don't need them. They would probably just say that you were too young to go, but I know different."

"I don't know—"

Decker narrowed his eyes. "Moonie, I happen to know that Gertie has been waiting for you for quite a long time. And you know what? Gus and Roo and Tank have kept quiet about it on purpose. I heard them talking. They want to keep you all to themselves."

"That's weird," Moon Pie said. "Why?"

"I don't know," Decker said. "Maybe they're bored. Maybe you're their entertainment. Like a little clown. All I know is, they *lied*. And so did Miss Lottie."

"I guess you're right," Moon Pie said softly. "I mean, if you just saw Gertie at the shelter . . ."

"Yes, I'm afraid it's true. Gertie has been waiting for you. I saw her myself, big glasses and all, and she misses you, Moonie. She misses you a lot."

Moon Pie's ears drooped. "I miss her, too."

"There, there," Decker said. He gave Moon Pie a lick on the top of his head. It was all he could do to keep himself from gagging. "Go to her tomorrow and everything will be okay. Don't tell anyone. Just slip out that hole and you'll be on your way."

Moon Pie stood. "I'll do it! I'll do it tomorrow!"

"Good for you, Moonie!"

Moon Pie started trotting back down the hall, then stopped. He turned.

"What if I can't remember how to get there?" he asked.

"Oh, you'll know," Decker said. "A good dog never forgets where his human lives."

Moon Pie's ears lifted. "You're right! I'll leave tomorrow! Thanks, Decker!"

"Of course," Decker said. "And remember! Don't tell anyone. They'll just try to keep you here. Now off you go."

Decker watched as Moon Pie hopped back down the hall to the family room. He cocked his head to one side. Sniffed the air.

"Cat, is that you I smell?"

The house was silent.

Decker sniffed harder. "Yes, yes it is." His growl was low and menacing. "Better keep your mouth shut."

He started walking down the hall, stopping every so often to sniff at corners.

"Because, cat, I have dealt with your kind before. And it wasn't pretty."

Ghost

Ghost listened from the shadows of the spare room as the new dog strutted down the hall. The white cat kept as still as possible.

Decker had threatened him. Again. This dog was bold. And unlike the others, he was unpredictable. Ghost fully believed that he had hurt many creatures in his past. He could sense this about Decker the same way he could sense a storm was coming.

Ghost could hear him lapping up water, then his big paws padding back down the hall. He paused outside the guest room.

"I mean it, cat," Decker said, before slipping into Miss Lottie's bedroom.

Ghost edged his way into the farthest corner of his under-bed home to think. He pulled Mouse into a one-paw hug and licked the top of his head twice quickly. Mouse, with his button eyes and string tail, soothed Ghost during times of turmoil.

He had indeed heard the conversation between Decker and Moon Pie. He had even crawled out from his lair so that he could hear better. He knew Decker had lied to the small dog. Gertie was dead, and they all knew it. All of them except Moon Pie. It was silly to keep her death from him, but dogs were silly in many ways.

Ghost didn't feel one way or the other about Moon Pie. He was just another noisy dog in a house full of noisy dogs. And Moon Pie was younger and bouncier and noisier than the others. Without him, the house would be quieter.

But Gus, well, that was different. Ghost liked the kindly terrier. And Gus would not want Moon Pie wandering around looking for his former human.

Ghost nipped Mouse's ear once. Hard.

Gus had initiated the Truce. And he had left Ghost two Tiddle Widdle Chicken Bits by the door that morning, as promised. He and Gus had had interesting discussions about life at Miss Lottie's, about the differences between cats and dogs, and about the oddness of people. They even had a silly, ongoing debate about which toys were better—tennis balls or balls of yarn.

As much as he hated to admit it, Ghost was lonely, and Gus made his life less so.

But more important, there was this new dog. Decker

didn't play by the rules of the pack. He would probably blatantly disregard the Truce, and without the Truce, Ghost was outnumbered. If all the dogs decided to listen to Decker, Ghost would have to find another home, and, well, he didn't even like coming out from under the bed, much less going outdoors to look for a new abode.

He licked Mouse's head, thinking.

He would do it. He would sneak into the family room, where the pack slept. Then he would quietly wake up Gus and tell him what Decker had said.

Ghost poked his nose out and sniffed nervously. He slipped out from under the bed. He would have to be extra quiet around this dangerous new dog.

He had explored the family room many times, but mostly when the dogs were asleep. Curling up under his bed day after day was boring, so he would investigate at night, being careful not to get too close to the sleeping dogs. He'd sniff at their food and bat at dangling things, like towels hanging over chairs or the string that pulled the shade down. But whenever he explored, he kept a good distance from the dogs. Gus, he trusted, but the rest, well . . .

There was no other way. He had to do this.

He sprinted down the hallway, keeping close to the wall, until he was standing in the entrance to the family room. The room was completely still except for the occasional snuffle or snore. He wove in and around the coffee table legs. Ghost could see Gus's scruffy silhouette in the dim light.

He trotted toward him quietly, stealthily, barely making a sound.

"Gus! Wake up! It's that spooky-scary cat!" cried Moon Pie.

Ghost froze. His muscles tightened. One ear twitched.

Gus raised his head. "Huh?"

Moon Pie started barking.

"Moonie, what's wrong?" Gus asked.

"The cat!" Moon Pie said. "The spooky-scary cat is here! He's here!"

"Whaaa—" Gus asked, shaking his head.

The next thing Ghost knew, Roo was standing up and barking. "WHAT'S GOING ON? IS THERE A FIRE? GUS, WHAT IS HAPPENING?"

"I don't know!" Gus said.

"Why don't you know, Gus?" Roo barked. "YOU NEVER KNOW!"

Moon Pie scrambled to his feet. "Go away!" he barked. He moved closer to Ghost, his teeth bared.

Ghost's heart slammed against his chest. "Be quiet!" he hissed. "You'll wake up the new dog!"

But Moon Pie only barked louder. "You're a sneak! That's what you are!" He moved closer to Ghost, snarling.

Ghost backed away. The dogs' barking grew more and

more frenzied. Once Ghost reached the doorway, he skittered out of the family room.

"Moonie, Roo, quiet!" Gus barked. "Everyone, shush!"

Roo and Moon Pie kept barking as Ghost scurried down the hall, slid under the bed, and curled up tightly with Mouse gripped between his paws. He could hear Miss Lottie's steps, followed by Decker's. Ghost held himself completely still.

"What's going on out here?" Miss Lottie said. The dogs stopped barking. Ghost heard Miss Lottie pour herself a glass of water. She heaved a sigh, then walked around a little while longer. "Okay," she said finally. "Everyone looks fine now."

She walked back down the hall with Decker at her side.

Ghost let out a lungful of air. Helping those silly dogs was too dangerous. They were on their own.

Ghost Before

He started life as Snowflake.
New homes meant new names.
Fluff (nah)
Snowball (yawn)
Marshmallow (never)
Lily (!)
Sam (almost)
Until finally
Lastly
Perfectly
Ghost (yes)
It didn't actually matter. He never came when he was called.

Roo

When Miss Lottie let them out for their morning pee, Roo waited until Decker walked out the back door first before following him into the yard. He was clearly the pack leader now, and she wanted to show him that she knew it.

It was *so, so* obvious to her. She couldn't understand why the other dogs didn't see it. Gus had lost this battle. It was as simple as that. When Decker had bitten his own paw, Gus didn't do ANYTHING.

HE NEVER DID ANYTHING.

Not when Ghost entered the living room the night before. Not when that rat got into the kitchen years ago. A RAT, for crying out loud! And Gus didn't do a thing! He just waited for Miss Lottie to take care of it. Ugh!

She was tired of the way Gus hesitated. Tired of the way he hemmed and hawed and waited until it was too late to make a good decision. Real leaders were decisive! They knew exactly what to do at all times! They didn't hang back, waiting for someone else to do the leading.

Gus was wishy-washy. Decker was confident. Strong. Brave.

Decker was everything that Gus was not. Decker was a leader.

Sure, biting himself was a strange thing to do. But Tank was such a bossypants, Roo couldn't blame Decker for getting him in trouble. And what better way to teach Tank that Decker was in charge now? It was actually the perfect move. After all, Decker didn't really hurt anyone but himself. It wasn't like he was mean.

The air had a wintery feel to it. Roo gave herself a shake. Next to her, Decker was sniffing a tree. She sidled up and sniffed it with him.

"Winter's on the way," Roo said.

Decker glanced back at her and then continued sniffing the tree.

"I personally don't mind winter," Roo continued. "It's better than summer. Summer's too hot, don't you think?"

Decker didn't seem to be paying much attention to her. Which was fine. As the new leader, he probably had bigger things on his mind than the weather.

"How do you like Miss Lottie's food?" Roo asked. "Are you getting enough treats?"

Decker stopped suddenly. He turned to look at her. "Not really," he said. "Maybe you should start giving me some of yours."

Roo hesitated. "Um, sure."

There was something about the request that didn't sit quite right with her, but leaders, Roo knew, needed their strength. If an extra treat would help Decker keep up his stamina, she would give it to him.

Decker sat. Roo quickly sat next to him. He was staring at Gus, so Roo did, too.

Gus had moseyed over to the back fence. He was gnawing on a stick. Again. If there were an award given to dogs for rock-and-stick-gnawing, Gus would get one. It was probably his dog gift, although frankly, it seemed like a useless one.

Of course, Gus was kind. He had helped her out a lot when she first moved into Miss Lottie's. He had woken her up when she had nightmares and given her an extra treat when she got nervous about something. And she had been nervous. A lot.

She wasn't really that nervous anymore. Not with Decker in charge.

Roo looked over at Decker and sighed. It felt comforting to have such a strong leader. She'd probably never be nervous about anything ever again.

"I love it in the yard, don't you?" Roo asked.

Decker looked at her but didn't say a word.

He was thinking big, important thoughts again, for sure.

Gus

Gus had been saving the stick, which was just crumbly enough to be satisfying, for a special occasion. A birthday, perhaps, or maybe a Thanksgiving treat. But now he simply gnawed on it while watching Roo. Every hair on his body stood at attention as he watched her follow Decker around the perimeter. She had been doing it all morning. If Decker sniffed a tree, she sniffed a tree. If he held his nose up to the sky, she did the same. It saddened Gus, and it made him worry.

And yet it didn't surprise him that Roo was acting this way. Soon after Roo arrived, a rat had gotten into Miss Lottie's kitchen, and Roo had frantically yelled at Gus to kill it.

"DO IT NOW!" she had yelled. Rats—like grasshoppers, vacuum cleaners, snowmen, lawnmowers, bathtubs, clowns, and motorcycles—were one of Roo's many fears.

But when Gus had looked into that rat's eyes, eyes that had pleaded with him, he just couldn't. Instead, he had barked until Miss Lottie rushed into the kitchen. She grabbed her broom and calmly brushed the rat out the back door, as if she were sweeping up a dust bunny.

Roo never looked at Gus the same way after that. In the span of a few minutes, their relationship had changed, and no matter what Gus did, he couldn't change it back. He could never make Roo feel safe.

And now Roo was ignoring him completely as she followed Decker to the stone birdbath. To follow another dog around like *he* was the pack leader was wrong, and Roo knew it.

Tank stood in the middle of the yard looking helpless and lost. Miss Lottie didn't trust him near the others yet, so she walked him on a leash while he did his business.

She gave the leash a tug. "Time to go in, boy."

Tank glanced at Decker before scooting inside.

Tank usually loved being in the yard. He would trot out happily, enjoying the good smells in the air. He'd dig for no apparent reason and bark at the squirrels on the fence. This new Tank hadn't even said hello.

Gus got up, made one circle, then another. He could not get comfortable. Something was bothering him even more than Roo and Tank. There was also the incident with Ghost the night before. It had seemed as though Ghost wanted to tell him something. It must have been important. Ghost usually only talked to Gus if Gus spoke to him first. His evening trip to the family room just didn't make sense.

Gus made another small circle. Sniffed the air. Put his head back on his paws.

What was it?

He realized with a start what it was. He hadn't seen Moon Pie in a while.

A long while.

Moon Pie

Moon Pie glanced around the yard. Gus was too busy chewing on a stick to notice him. Roo was following Decker around. Tank had barely looked at him before being dragged back inside with Miss Lottie.

Moon Pie casually sniffed at one of the bushes in front of the hole so that he could get a better look at it. It was a big hole—definitely big enough for him to escape.

He could do it! He could slip through and go looking for Gertie! It would only take a second. He'd run off and find Gertie's house and then he'd be back with her again.

He could see it all in his mind's eye. Gertie's happy smile when she saw him. Gertie swinging him through the air again and feeding him popcorn and watching TV with him. His heart felt all thumpy at the thought of being with his old Gertie again.

Decker gave Moon Pie a sidelong glance. He nodded and firmly wagged his tail once.

Moon Pie knew what that meant. Now was the time. If he stood there any longer, he might lose his nerve.

He darted into the thick patch of trees and bushes. A branch scratched his ear. It was all he could do not to yelp. He wiggled his way through until the hole was right in front of him.

He paused. He could see through the hole to the alley beyond.

What if he couldn't find Gertie?

What if he got lost forever and ever?

What if he was eaten by coyotes?

"Moon Pie? Where are you?"

Gus was calling him. He had to leave *now*.

Moon Pie held his breath.

"You can do it!" he whispered.

He carefully put his front paws through the opening and slipped through the hole.

It was easy, just like Decker had said!

Moon Pie ran down the alley without looking back. He knew that if he did, he might change his mind.

Gus

Moon Pie had been acting strange all morning. Instead of running and chasing Roo as he usually did, he had quietly done his business by the birdbath. Gus had been distracted by Tank and had lost track of Moonie.

"Moon Pie? Where are you?" Gus called.

Roo glanced over at Gus, then went back to following Decker around.

Gus got to his feet and scanned the yard. He wandered over to the porch and looked underneath it. Sometimes Moon Pie liked to snoop under there.

"Moon Pie?"

Gus peered into the darkness. Moon Pie loved to hide, but he was a snorting, snuffling kind of dog and was easy to find just by the noises he made. The space under the porch was quiet and empty.

Gus's heart beat faster. He trotted over to the long, narrow strip of grass along the side of the house. A gate there led to the front yard. Occasionally Quinn or Miss Lottie left the gate open, but it was shut tight.

There was only one other place he might have gone.

Gus ran over to the patch of bushes and fir trees that stood in the corner of the yard.

"Moon Pie?"

Gus had only been in there once before, and had come out with dozens of small scratches. He braced himself and went in.

The sharp, scraggly branches on the bushes scraped his sides. Once he was inside, he could see that two of the slats in the fence had rotted away and fallen to the ground, making a hole big enough for a small dog to fit through.

Gus backed out quickly, butt first. He winced when the branches scratched him again. He charged across the yard and stood in front of Roo.

"Everyone! Come here! Moon Pie is gone!"

"WHAT? WHERE DID HE GO? HOW LONG AGO? ARE YOU SURE?"

Roo started running in circles.

"Roo, stop!" Decker said.

Roo slowed, then stopped. She looked down at the

ground, panting, then glanced up at Decker.

"Roo, Decker!" Gus barked. "We need to get out there and look for Moon Pie right now!"

Decker sat down and casually tugged at his bandage with his teeth. "Why?"

"Because he's loose and he's young and he doesn't know how to be on his own, that's why!" Gus said.

"So?" Decker asked.

Gus growled. "We are a pack. Packs help each other."

"We'd probably just get lost, too." Decker stood and yawned. "Besides, how do you know what's best? Maybe he's better off on his own."

Gus's fur tingled. He growled. "You obviously don't understand what it means to be a good pack member." He glanced over at Roo. "We don't have time for this! Come on, Roo! You're the best tracker I know!"

Roo started chasing her tail. "I think—I mean, I know—I mean, I think—" She stopped and looked at Decker, who was staring at her. "I'm staying with Decker."

Gus shook his head. He wasn't sure he'd heard her right. "*What?*" he asked.

"He knows what's best." She put her head down and scampered into the corner of the yard.

Gus didn't have time to think about what Roo had just said. He ran to the back door. He barked and pawed at it until Miss Lottie appeared.

"What in heaven's name is wrong with you, Gus? Is it that important that you come in?" She opened the door for him, but he barked and walked backward, toward the fence.

"I don't know what you want," Miss Lottie said. She came out into the yard and looked around. "What is it? A squirrel?" Miss Lottie put one hand on her hip and raised the other to shield her eyes from the sun.

"I don't see what you're—hey, wait a minute, where's Moon Pie?"

Gus gave one sharp bark and raced over to the firs. He stood by them and barked.

"Is he over there? Is he in the bushes? Oh, gosh, how will we ever get him out?" Miss Lottie said as she hobbled over to Gus. Once she got to him, she bent down and looked into the bushes

"I don't see him." She groaned as she got down on her knees to look more closely. "Moon Pie? Are you there—oh NO!" She stood. "There's a hole!"

Gus had never seen Miss Lottie move so quickly. She raced over to the gate, threw it open, and ran out into the alley. "Moon Pie! Moon Pie! Here, boy!"

Gus stood by the gate. He barked as he stared through the fence and watched anxiously as Miss Lottie jogged down the alley calling for the small dog.

Moon Pie, the youngest and most vulnerable member

of his pack, was loose in the alley. Without Tank watching over him, he could get into all kinds of trouble. Cars, trucks, wild animals.

Everything out there posed a danger to the little pug.

Gus

Miss Lottie strode back into the yard, shaking her head.

"I should have checked that fence, I should have known that hole was there," she mumbled. "Come on, kiddos!" She waved the dogs toward the back door. "We're all going inside."

Once she was in the kitchen, Miss Lottie pulled her cell phone from her jeans pocket and punched in a number.

"Quinn, I've got bad news," she said quickly. "Moon Pie is gone. He escaped through a hole in the fence. Can you ride your bike around, see if you can find him?" She nodded as he responded. "Thanks," she said. "I'll make a few calls from my end."

While she started calling neighbors, Gus trotted over to

the laundry room. Tank was curled up in his kennel again, with his back facing the room.

"Tank, Tank, wake up!"

"Hmmmm . . ."

"It's Moon Pie. He's gone."

Tank's ears sprang straight up. "What?!"

"There's a hole in the fence, by the fir trees. He must have gone through it."

Tank struggled to stand on his short, stocky legs. He turned around to face Gus. "Why? What got into him? Haven't we told him not to go there?"

"I guess he didn't listen," Gus said. "He's young."

Tank snorted. "It's that new dog! I bet he had something to do with it! Ever since he came here—"

"You need to help me find Moonie," Gus said.

Tank's ears drooped. He sighed. "I don't know," he said quietly. "I just don't know."

"What do you mean?"

"I don't see how I can help."

Gus stared at his friend. "Tank, you are my top dog. My go-to guy. I need your help. I don't care what Miss Lottie says. I know you're a good dog and I know you are the best dog to help me. Besides, it's Moon Pie. He trusts you more than anyone."

Tank looked down at the floor. "I don't know. I'm—"

"We are a pack, and you are coming with me!" Gus said.

"We need to find Moonie!"

Tank stared at Gus for a moment. "Okay . . . okay. I will." He heaved his big body out of his kennel and gave himself a shake from head to tail.

"Good. Now we need to think of how to get out there to find him."

Ghost's scent hit both dogs at the same time.

Gus spun around.

Tank barked once, loudly.

Ghost stood in the doorway of the laundry room flicking his tail.

"If you had just listened to me last night, this whole thing never would have happened," Ghost said.

Tank growled.

"Stop, Tank," Gus said. "Remember the Truce."

Ghost sat and curled his tail around his feet. "I tried telling you, Gus."

"Telling me what?"

"Yeah, telling Gus what, cat?" Tank asked, growling.

"Forget it," Ghost said. "I don't need this."

He turned and strode out of the room with his tail high.

"Wait!" Gus said, chasing after him.

The white cat trotted down the hall and into the guest room. Gus raced after him and watched as he slithered under the bed. Gus took a few careful steps toward him.

"Tell me what?" Gus asked.

"Nothing. Goodbye."

"Did you hear something last night? Something with Moon Pie and the new dog?"

Silence.

Gus sat. He scratched himself behind the ear and thought.

"I'm sorry Moon Pie called you spooky and scary," Gus said. "He shouldn't have done that. He doesn't know you like I do, and he's afraid of things he doesn't know."

Gus couldn't see what Ghost was doing, but he could feel it in an animal way. He could feel Ghost pivoting his ears toward him. He could feel him twitching his nose.

"And I'm sorry Roo barked at you. I know you hate it when she barks. I'll have a talk with her and Moon Pie. And Tank."

Ghost's white nose poked out from beneath the bed. "Your pack is utterly deranged. What a commotion! You'd think they'd never seen a cat before."

"They're just . . . dogs," Gus said. "You know how we can be."

"Boorish?" Ghost asked.

"Yes," Gus said.

"Ignorant? Loud? Uncouth?"

"Yes, yes, and yes," Gus said. He ground his teeth. It wasn't easy coming down so hard on his pack, but he knew Ghost was partly right.

"There was something you wanted to tell me last night," Gus continued. He paused, taking his time. "Was it about Moon Pie? Is that why you came to see me?"

Ghost's nose went back under the bed. "You mean when your pack insulted me?"

Gus chose his next words carefully. "Come on. We're friends. At least, that's what I've always thought. Please don't let the others come between us."

The pause seemed to last forever. Gus nervously gnawed at his side. They needed to be out there searching for Moon Pie. Miss Lottie was only human. Her search techniques would be limited. Gus knew this particular search required a dog's senses.

Ghost slipped out from underneath the bed and faced Gus.

"You dogs can be so dense."

"I know," Gus said.

Ghost sat. His odd owlish eyes stared at Gus. "The little one, Moon Pie, talked to the new dog last night in the hallway," Ghost said.

Gus pricked up his ears. "And? What did he say?"

"The new dog said that Gertie was waiting for him. He said that you and Roo and Tank had all lied and that she's been waiting for him at her house all along. Then he told Moon Pie he could escape through the hole in the fence."

Gus felt a burst of anger deep inside his throat. He

growled. "I can't believe it! That's so wrong! How could Decker do that?"

"Believe it," Ghost said. "Your little Moon Pie is on his way to his old house."

"Oh no," Gus said. "This is bad."

"Yeah, well, I thought you should know," Ghost said. He started to make his way back under the bed.

"Ghost?"

"Yes?"

"I really appreciate it."

Ghost blinked at Gus before slipping back under the bed.

"If there's anything you ever need—" Gus began.

"I'm really not spooky or bad," Ghost said from his lair. "Maybe you could tell your pack that."

"I will," Gus said. "I promise."

But first he needed to find Moon Pie.

Moon Pie

Minutes after he sprinted out of the hole, Moon Pie heard Miss Lottie calling him.

"Moon Pie! Moooooon Pie!"

Moon Pie glanced to his left. An open garage! He dashed inside and curled up tight under a crumpled tarp that lay in the corner.

Miss Lottie's voice sounded sad and desperate, but he stayed hidden. She could look for him as long as she wanted to. He was never going back to her. Not ever. She had *stolen* him. Stolen him away from Gertie and the home he loved.

As soon as Miss Lottie stopped calling him, Moon Pie got up, gave himself a shake, and went back into the alley. He sniffed the air.

He smelled grass and pavement and rakes and bunnies. And . . . something else. Something that bothered him.

He sniffed again, harder this time. He knew that was what hunting dogs did. They smelled the air for danger. Gus had told him all about it.

Gus. Moon Pie had loved him almost as much as he loved Gertie, but Gus had lied to him. Roo, too. Worst of all was Tank.

Moon Pie whimpered, thinking of Tank. His favorite pack member! How could he lie? It didn't make sense.

Moon Pie shook his head, hoping he could clear it of all the angry thoughts he had. Any second now he would smell something that would remind him of home, just like a real live hunting dog. Any second now he would find his old Gertie, too. Any second!

That smell was back. It was dark and heavy. His fur prickled.

He growled his fiercest growl.

All was quiet.

"Moon Pie! Where are you?!"

Quinn. At the end of the block. He wished they would all just quit looking for him so he could get on with his adventure! Moon Pie dashed back into the garage and made himself as small as possible. He couldn't see Quinn, but he could hear him riding closer.

"Moon Pie! Mooooon Piiie! Want a treat? Wherever you are, if you come out, I'll give you a treat!"

A treat sounded good. A treat sounded very good. He

tilted his head to one side, thinking.

The first thought that came to him was Gertie. And popcorn. And her big, big bed. She was all alone and she needed him. He curled into a tighter ball.

"Moon Pie? Moonie? Are you here?"

Moon Pie could hear the tires on Quinn's bike whir as he rode down the alley. The whirring sound got farther and farther away.

Moon Pie stayed in the garage for a long time. He stared out at the alley and watched as the light grew dimmer. When he left Miss Lottie's the sun had been high in the sky. Now it sat on top of the trees. Soon it would be dark, and he was still only four houses down from Miss Lottie's.

When he was sure both Miss Lottie and Quinn were gone, Moon Pie crawled out of his hiding spot and stood in the middle of the alley, looking at the end of it. The last few rays of sunlight stretched across the pavement.

He wasn't sure what to do next. He had escaped, and he had successfully hidden from both Miss Lottie and Quinn. But now what? He decided to head toward the yellow house at the end of the street. It was on the opposite end from Miss Lottie's house, which felt safer, somehow. He needed to get far away from her and the others.

He liked traveling by alley. There were so many interesting things to eat! He found a pizza crust, a hamburger bun, and, best of all, tater tots. Everything was so much better than the dry kibble Miss Lottie made them eat. He almost got a doughnut, too, except a creepy squirrel snagged it first.

The bad smell wafted his way again. Was it just an especially creepy squirrel? He knew squirrels couldn't really hurt him. But still. He didn't like that smell at all.

When he finally got to the end of the alley, he sat. Gertie had trained him to sit before crossing the street. He wasn't really sure when he should cross. Miss Lottie and Gertie always seemed to know exactly when to do it.

A car whizzed by. He felt its wind push against his fur. He had never crossed the street by himself, but if he ran really fast, it should be fine. How hard could it be?

He sighed. Maybe this was not such a great idea. Maybe he needed Miss Lottie to help him find Gertie's house.

The sun had almost set. He needed to go soon.

The sound of dry leaves scraping the pavement made him jump.

And the smell. Something was close. Something bad.

It wasn't squirrels.

He needed to go *now*!

He held his breath as he sprinted toward the other side of the street. His heart banged in his chest, and his legs pumped faster and faster.

He was almost there when he heard a long, loud *screeeeech*.

Gus

For most of the day, Gus and Tank stood by the back door waiting to be let out. They had both barked and pawed at the door earlier, but Miss Lottie had shouted at them so sharply, they had kept quiet.

Quinn and Miss Lottie were slumped at the kitchen table. Before them were two plates of uneaten grilled-cheese sandwiches and two bowls of untouched tomato soup. Quinn poked at his phone. Miss Lottie fiddled with her soupspoon.

Decker got off the couch in the family room and went over to Miss Lottie. He gave her elbow a nudge with his nose. When she looked down he licked her hand.

"Aw, thank you," she said to him.

"What a fake," Tank said.

Decker sauntered back to the couch. He gave Roo one quick glance before he hopped onto it. Roo got up and pushed her bed closer to the couch with her nose.

Tank grunted.

"What's with Roo?" he asked. "She's been following Decker all day."

"Who knows?" Gus said. "She never did like me as pack leader."

The thought that he had disappointed Roo so much that she had started following Decker made Gus feel heavy and worn out. He needed to get his pack back together again. They couldn't splinter off like this. It wasn't how packs were meant to be.

Miss Lottie picked up her sandwich, put it back down. "Did you look near Foster?" she asked Quinn. "The yellow house at Foster and Orrington? They've got a lot of junk in their backyard. He might have snuck in there."

Quinn nodded. "I looked. I went down every alley in the neighborhood."

Miss Lottie picked up her sandwich again, then dropped it, her eyes widening. "Moon Pie has old tags on! With Gertie's address and phone number! If someone finds him, they won't be able to call me. Oh, what an idiot I am." She pushed her plate away. "I don't know when I can get that fence fixed. And if I don't, I'm afraid I'll lose another dog."

Quinn shook his head. "I don't think so," he said. "I've

never seen any of the other dogs interested in that part of the yard. Plus, I don't even think they could fit."

"I suppose." Miss Lottie nodded absently. "We'll need to put up some fliers with Moonie's picture."

"I have one of him," Quinn said. "I can do that."

They ate in silence. Gus gave a soft woof.

"Well, all right then," Miss Lottie said. She got up from the table, walked over to the back door, and opened it for the two dogs. "Out you go. Quinn, can you make sure they don't escape through that hole?"

"Sure," Quinn said. He grabbed his sandwich and headed out after the dogs.

"Now what?" Tank said. He paused by the dying rosebush. "How are we going to ditch Quinn?"

"We'll wait until he's not watching," Gus said. "You know he's always looking at his phone. Maybe we can sneak out then."

The two dogs wandered around the yard, occasionally glancing over their shoulders to watch Quinn, who sat on an old plastic chair eating his sandwich. Sure enough, once he was finished with the sandwich, Quinn took his phone from his back pocket.

"This is it," Gus said. His heart beat faster. "Let's go over there slowly and quietly."

Tank crawled into the thick bushes first, with Gus right behind him.

"Ow! These branches!" Tank said.

"I know, keep going," Gus said.

Tank let out a few more quiet yips and yaps until they reached the hole.

"I can't fit through there," Tank said.

"Here, I'll go first. Maybe I can push these other boards farther apart," Gus said.

Gus poked his head and forepaws through the fence and leaned against one board. It bit into his skin, moving slightly. He leaned harder against the other. It budged! He pushed through, then turned to face Tank.

"Come on! I made the hole bigger! You can do it!"

Tank looked at the hole and shook his head. "I don't think so—"

"Gus? Tank? Where are you guys?"

"Hurry!" Gus said.

Gus heard Quinn's sneakers thudding against the ground as he ran to the back of the yard.

Tank grunted, then plowed through the fence, full force.

Craaaack!

"AROOO!"

Tank smashed through, taking one of the slats with him. He stood in front of Gus, panting.

"You okay?" Gus asked.

"I dunno," Tank said. He looked at his left side. A trickle of blood ran down it. "I—"

"Stay! STAY!" Quinn yelled from the yard.

"Let's go!" Gus said.

They raced into the alley with Quinn's yells echoing in their ears.

Quinn would get in trouble for this, but that didn't matter now. All that mattered was finding Moon Pie.

Quinn

Quinn threw open the gate and sprinted into the alley. He stopped in the middle of it. His head whipped from one side to the other, searching for Gus and Tank.

He hadn't been fast enough. They were either hiding or halfway down the alley.

He hopped on his bike, heart pounding. His face was hot, and his eyes were blurry from tears. He didn't bother wiping them away. It didn't matter who saw him crying. Nothing mattered now except getting those dogs back.

"Gus, Tank! Come out!"

It was his fault. All of it. If he hadn't been checking his stupid phone, this never would have happened. Miss Lottie had asked him to watch the dogs, and he had failed.

Maybe what Jessie and his friends said about him was

true. He *was* worthless. Maybe he *had* been the one who let go of Murph's leash.

He choked back more tears. "Come on, you guys! Please?"

He pedaled up and down the alley with wild thoughts buzzing in his brain.

He would have to tell Miss Lottie. She would be so upset. Three of her precious dogs were gone. He wouldn't blame her if she fired him.

What would his mom say?

More important, what would Jessie say?

And what if they were in danger? If what his mom said was true, and there really was a coyote around, would the dogs be able to protect themselves?

He thought of Moon Pie, so tiny and helpless. He should have told Miss Lottie about the coyote. She would have made sure her backyard was safe. She would have fixed the fence.

But then another thought struck him. Why didn't *he* fix the fence? He knew there might be a coyote in the neighborhood, and yet he let himself get sucked into those dumb texts instead of fixing the hole. All it needed were a few boards nailed across it. Why didn't he think to do it himself?

He rode this way for what seemed like hours. Every once in a while he got off his bike to peer behind a garage, but they weren't there.

He pulled out his phone to check the time. He had been searching the alley for twenty minutes, but really, he had no idea if the dogs were even still there. By now Miss Lottie probably would have noticed that he and the dogs weren't in the yard. She'd be looking for them.

He had to go back. He had to tell her.

He pedaled slowly, still inspecting every yard, every garage, every shed.

They were gone.

Miss Lottie stood waiting by the gate.

"Quinn, what happened? Where is everyone?" she called to him.

He shook his head and pedaled faster until he was right in front of her. Miss Lottie's cheeks were flushed. She stared at him with wide eyes.

"Please don't tell me—" she said.

He nodded. "I'm so sorry. They both got out."

"Oh no." Miss Lottie grabbed on to the wooden fence and held it tightly with both hands. "This is awful, just awful," she said, her voice trembling. "What are we going to do?"

She was asking Quinn for an answer. An answer to a problem he had created.

He hated seeing her this way, all twisted and worried. "I'll find them," Quinn said. "I promise."

And even though the words sounded confident coming out of his mouth, Quinn doubted that he could do it.

He was exactly what his brother said he was. Useless.

Decker

Decker wandered over to the metal bowl and gulped down the rest of the water. Once he was finished, he ate the remaining food in all five bowls.

He gazed at the bed near the TV. It was big and thick. It used to be Gus's, but Gus wouldn't be back. He was a weak leader, obviously, and now he and the others were off on a wild-goose chase. Those stupid mutts would get lost in their own backyard.

Decker had never felt this relaxed. It had been so *easy*. The only one left now was the crazy three-legged dog, and she was behaving well. He could probably get her to give him most of her food and her treats. He'd keep her around for now.

Oh, and the cat. But Decker was sure he could keep Ghost out of his way. If not, well, he was just a cat and, from what Decker had heard, not a very big one.

This was the way life was meant to be. Of course he should get the tastiest treats and the best beds and the most attention from Miss Lottie. He was bigger and stronger than all the others. He sighed blissfully and collapsed onto the bed.

"I knew that would happen, Quinn!" Miss Lottie said. "I knew we were asking for trouble with that hole!"

Miss Lottie had not stopped pacing since she came back into the house.

"I'm sorry," Quinn said for the third time. He was sitting at the kitchen table with his head in his hands. "I tried to catch them, but they were too fast."

Miss Lottie had called all her neighbors, as well as the pound and the shelter. Decker wished she would stop. It would be so inconvenient to have those mutts come back just when he'd gotten rid of them.

"I don't understand it," Miss Lottie said. She slid her phone back into her pocket and ran shaky fingers through her hair. "I've heard of dogs having problems with new members being introduced to the pack, but this is too much!"

"It's all my fault," Quinn said. He wiped his nose with the back of his hand and stared intently at a napkin on the table. "I'm really, really sorry. I should have fixed that stupid hole."

Miss Lottie stopped pacing. She sighed and ruffled

Quinn's hair. "Oh, honey, you couldn't have known they'd escape that way. This is so unlike them!" She shook her head. "Besides, between the two of us, we'll find them. First we really should move something in front of that hole so that no one else can escape."

Quinn frowned.

"I don't know," he said. "What if they come back and they can't get in?"

Miss Lottie nodded. "You're right. You're a smart kid. I guess we'll just have to keep these two tied up when they're outside," she said, gesturing at Roo and Decker.

Roo lifted her head. "Tied up? TIED UP?" She stood quickly. "They want to tie us up? They can't tie us up. Why would they—"

Decker growled softly so that Quinn and Miss Lottie couldn't hear. "Be. Quiet."

Roo clamped her jaw shut. She eyed Decker as she walked cautiously over to the food bowls.

"There's nothing left." She stood over the bowls, looking from one to the other. "You ate everything *and* drank all the water."

"So?"

"Nothing, it's just that—"

"Listen. Things will be different now. You'll eat when I tell you to. You'll drink when I tell you to. And you'll sleep where I tell you to. Got it?"

Roo blinked and looked at the floor.

"Got it," she said.

"Now get back on your bed and be quiet."

"Okay," Roo said. She slunk over to her bed and curled up on it. But she kept her eyes on him.

Decker nestled in. "This bed is perfect," he said. "It's so big." He stretched his legs out straight in front of him. "Don't even think of sleeping on it."

Roo was quiet. She stared at him with a strange look in her eyes.

"Did you hear me?" he asked.

"Yes," she said finally. "I understand."

She got up and turned around so that she wasn't facing him.

Perhaps she wasn't as easy as he thought. Perhaps he'd have to get rid of her, too.

Gus

Gus and Tank managed to avoid Quinn by hiding behind an old mattress leaning up against a garage. Every time he got close, they'd quietly scooted away from him into the shadows. They stayed there for a long time, listening to him riding up and down, up and down. Once they heard Miss Lottie's back gate close, they cautiously crawled out from their hiding place.

"Now what?" Tank asked. He licked a drop of blood off his side.

"Are you sure you can do this?" Gus asked. "That looks bad."

"Are you kidding?" Tank asked. "This is nothing. I'm tougher than a few scratches."

Tank was right. Even though he was old, he was still the toughest dog in the pack.

Gus held Tank's gaze. "Ghost told me that Decker and Moon Pie talked last night. Decker told Moonie that Gertie was still alive and that she was waiting for him."

"He WHAT?" Tank's fur stood on end. He growled.

"He also said that we lied to Moonie about Gertie being on vacation," Gus added.

Tank growled again. "I'm going to bite that Decker right in the—"

"No," Gus said. "You won't. That's not going to help. And besides, I did lie to Moonie. I should have told him Gertie was dead. I should have told him the truth."

Tank hesitated. "I suppose. But I didn't want him to know the truth, either. It would make him so sad."

"Maybe being sad is okay," Gus said. When his family didn't come looking for him, Gus thought he would be sad for the rest of his life. But he had found happiness again with Miss Lottie. His sadness had made him stronger simply because he now knew he could survive it. Moon Pie would survive it, too. "What's important now is that we find Moonie and bring him back home. If he thinks that Gertie is out there looking for him, he might do something stupid."

"How? I don't know where Moonie used to live, do you?"

"No. But I kind of doubt he'd know how to get there, either. He's practically a puppy. Let's see if we can get a trace of his scent, then go from there."

Gus put his head to the ground and started sniffing,

but his nose had never been very good. He could smell the coldness of the pavement if he pressed his nose right up against it. He could also smell the faint remnants of Chinese food and earthworms.

And then something else.

A dark, heavy smell wafted past him for a moment, then it was gone.

"Do you smell something?" he asked Tank. "Something, I don't know, dangerous?"

Tank paused and sniffed.

"Nope," Tank said. "Don't smell Moon Pie, either."

Tank's nose was even worse than Gus's. The one with the best nose was Roo, who was part hunting dog. Although some of the pack thought Roo's dog gift was her speed, Gus had always thought it was her ability to catch a scent. He and Tank joked that she could probably track down a baby mouse nestled in a leaf two houses away.

Roo would have smelled that bad scent. She would have known right away if it was something to worry about.

Gus shook his head. Roo had stayed behind because *he* wasn't a strong enough leader. It was his fault that she wasn't there with them right now.

The air grew colder. Tank's breathing was labored.

"Let's rest," Gus said.

"I'm not tired! I could go for hours!"

Gus scanned the edges of the alley, looking for a soft, safe spot they could curl up in. The dangerous smell was completely gone. They were safe for now.

A garage stood open to his right. He wandered in and noticed a crumpled-up tarp in the corner. It was perfect for a short nap.

"We won't be much good for anything if we don't get some rest," Gus said. "Come on, buddy."

"I suppose," Tank said. He sniffed around an old bucket.

Gus sighed before lying down. He was more tired than he thought, and the tarp was surprisingly comfortable.

Immediately he picked up the faintest whiff of . . . something. A good something. It was familiar to Gus, as familiar as Miss Lottie's laundry detergent or Quinn's peanut butter sandwiches.

Gus looked up at the ceiling, thinking. He took another sniff.

Popcorn!

Moon Pie!

"Tank, I think I smell Moonie!"

Tank charged over to him, huffing with each step. He bent his head down low to get a good sniff.

"That's Moonie, all right! Let's look in the yard!"

The two dogs raced out of the garage and into the yard behind it. They sniffed behind bushes, under a porch, next to a garden hose. Everywhere they thought Moon Pie might be.

"I think we're wasting our time here," Gus said. "Moonie might have looked around a bit to see if there was food here, but then he'd leave. This yard is too boring for him."

Tank swung his head as he looked from one side of the alley to the other. "Let's go," he said.

Just as he reached the edge of the yard, Gus stopped. His ears twitched involuntarily. Strange sounds were coming from the end of the alley. He could hear panting and nails against pavement.

"Do you hear that?" he asked Tank.

"Yup."

They trotted into the alley and looked to the right. The sun had set, making it difficult to see what was coming at them in the moonlight.

Gus squinted. A few houses down, he could see an animal that was close to their size.

It was loping toward them.

It definitely wasn't a dog. Not loose in the alley like that without its human.

Which meant it was probably a coyote. He had seen them on and off over the years, poking around Miss Lottie's garbage pails, or sniffing the back fence. They were never a welcome sight.

Coyotes had a bad reputation in the animal kingdom. They were fearless. Mean-spirited. An enemy to all dogs. Especially small dogs.

Like Moon Pie.

Gus knew at that moment that the dark, heavy scent he had picked up earlier was coyote.

Gus's fur bristled. "Tank, don't move—"

Tank gave a sharp bark and started running toward the coyote.

"Tank, stop!" Gus yelled.

But Tank kept charging down the alley, Gus at his heels.

Moon Pie

The screeching sound seemed to last forever.

Moon Pie froze. It was so loud! Like nothing he had ever heard before. He was too afraid to turn toward it.

He should never have left Miss Lottie's. Something bad was happening and he didn't know what to do! He squeezed his eyes shut, hoping that whatever it was would go away.

Then the air changed. Moon Pie felt a warmth all over his body, like he was bundled up in blankets on Gertie's big bed. The warmth spread across his fur and burrowed its way into his heart. For a moment he wasn't afraid.

He opened his eyes. A voice whispered in his ear.

RUN, Moon Pie, RUN!

Moon Pie did what the voice said. His paws skittered across the pavement. He felt a swoosh of wind and smelled a sharp, smoky odor.

When he reached the other side of the street he stopped and looked back. A car had pulled over. A woman got out.

"Oh my God! Are you okay? You poor little thing!"

She walked slowly over to Moon Pie and smiled as she reached down to pick him up.

Moon Pie hesitated. The woman looked nice enough, and she smelled toasty and delicious, like warm pudding and muffins.

Maybe one quick cuddle. He took a step toward her.

"Good boy!"

Moon Pie stopped. He didn't have time for cuddles with strangers, even if she did smell like warm pudding and muffins. He was close to finding Gertie, he just knew it!

The lady's fingertips brushed his sides as he scampered away. He ran down the sidewalk as fast as he could while the woman called "Here, boy!" behind him.

As much as he hated to run away from the nice-smelling lady, Gertie needed him. Soon he would be on the big bed eating popcorn, and everything would be just as it was.

He slowed down to a fast walk. It was completely dark except for the lights mounted above the garages in the alley. They were bright, but not bright enough to calm his fears.

He thought about the voice that had whispered in his ear. It had sounded so familiar, even though it was faint. He stopped for a moment so he could think even harder.

The voice had sounded like *Gertie*. But how could that

be? He hadn't seen her or smelled her. He thought about the warmth he had felt, like he was up on the big bed.

Maybe she had been there but he hadn't seen her. Which seemed very weird. If it was true, though, she was close! She was probably playing some kind of hide-and-seek game.

Moon Pie paused. Something else was close. Watching him.

It could be his imagination. Gus often told him that he had a big imagination. That there were no sneaky-pete mice at Miss Lottie's.

"You're letting your imagination run away with you again," Gus would say.

Still. Moon Pie felt a tremble deep inside his belly.

He barked once, loudly, then looked around. It was dark and scary.

"Come out! I'm not scared of you!"

This wasn't true, not at all, but he thought now was a good time for lying.

The alley was quiet. Too quiet.

He walked slowly down the street, peering into the darkness. Oh, Gertie, Gertie, Gertie. Why wasn't she here when he needed her? She always had been in the past. Always.

A good smell beckoned him. A cheesy, melty smell. With bacon!

Moon Pie's ears stood up. He tilted his head to the sky and sniffed hard, his mouth slightly open. The cheesy, melty bacon smell was close! He took a few steps toward it, holding his head high. His stomach rumbled. He was getting very, very close. It seemed to be coming from a yard to his left. He sniffed as he walked closer.

Pizza. Definitely pizza. With melty cheese and bacon.

He stopped. Was that a grumble? Something soft and low? Like someone else's empty stomach?

Moon Pie didn't wait to see what it might be. He raced toward the smell, ears flapping in the cold night air. He barked a few loud yaps to scare whatever it was away.

He came to the edge of a yard that was crowded with interesting things, like boxes and tires and an old swing set. He liked this yard very much.

An overstuffed trash can stood near the house. Perched on top of it was a pizza box. There was definitely still pizza in there, he was sure of it.

All he needed to do was bump into the trash can and knock off that pizza box.

It would be so easy.

He walked slowly into the yard, careful not to make a noise. He was a ninja dog—a ninja dog on a mission for pizza.

A strange sound caught his attention. A scratching sound. He looked around, but the yard was still.

The cheesy, melty bacon smell was stronger now. So strong, he couldn't resist it. He would run right into the trash can, knock it over with his paws, grab the pizza, and run back into the best-lit part of the alley to eat it.

Moon Pie liked this plan. It seemed brave and daring. He had often listened to the stories Roo told about living on the streets. It all sounded so exciting and adventurous.

Well, he was having his own adventure. He couldn't wait to tell the others about it!

Except that he wouldn't be telling them. He was probably never going to see them again.

His thoughts turned back to the pizza as the smell wafted his way, making a path straight to his nose. He took two steps backward to give himself a running start, then he rammed into the trash can, slamming his paws against it.

The scratching, scrabbling sound grew louder. Moon Pie backed up and hit the trash can again. This time, he heard the box sliding off the top. He looked up in time to see it falling toward him.

He also saw something else falling with it.

"Wha—"

By the time he figured out what had happened, it was too late.

Gus

Gus panted as he ran.

"Wait, Tank—"

Tank didn't slow down. He kept running toward the strange animal.

"Tank, don't!"

The coyote stopped. Tank rushed up to him. Gus watched in fear as the coyote lifted his head and howled.

Gus knew that howl. It wasn't a coyote at all.

"Roo!" Gus said, running toward her.

Tank gently headbutted the three-legged dog.

"Roo!" he said. "You came back to us!"

"WHAT ARE YOU GUYS DOING? WHERE'S MOON PIE? HAVE YOU FOUND HIM?"

Roo spun around four times quickly.

"Slow down, Roo," Gus warned. "You'll make yourself dizzy."

"You came back," Tank said again. "You didn't desert us after all."

Roo looked down at the ground. "I'm sorry. I really really really am. I shouldn't have followed that Decker." She gave herself a big shake. "I thought I'd be better off with him. Safer, maybe. But all he cares about is himself. Not like you, Gus. You always put us first." She bowed her head and looked up at him. "I'm sorry."

"It's okay," Gus said. He nuzzled her with his nose. "How did you get out?"

"As soon as Miss Lottie opened the back door for my pee, I ran and I ran and I ran and I ran until I got to that hole! I blasted right through it!"

"Good job, Roo!" Tank said.

Gus wagged his tail. "So you'll help us find Moon Pie?"

"Absolutely positively I will!" Roo said. She spun twice for emphasis.

"Good," Gus said. "Because we haven't had any luck. We know he's trying to get back to Gertie, but we also know he probably doesn't know how to find her. We smell him here." Gus nodded toward the garage. "But we don't know where he went next."

Roo gave herself a shake. She sat down, flattened her ears against her head, and lifted her nose to the sky. "He's not far," she said. Like all dogs, when she was doing what she was born to do—which in Roo's case was tracking— she was calm, confident, and focused. "Not far at all." She got up and started heading down the alley with her nose to the ground. "Follow me."

Gus and Tank followed Roo. She wove in and out of every yard, sometimes sniffing hard, sometimes looking up with a wondering expression.

"I think he found a snack, so he isn't starving," she said.

"I was never worried about Moon Pie starving," Gus said. "He could find a treat on Mars."

Roo kept sniffing at the grass, the pavement, the garbage. She went farther and farther down the alley until she found something that made her sniff harder.

"I smell smoke," she said.

"Smoke?" Gus asked.

"Yes, like from a car."

She trotted to the end of the alley. "And I smell Moonie." She closed her eyes, then opened them again. "And . . ."

"Yes?" Gus asked. Although he was pretty sure he knew what she was going to say.

"I smell coyote," she said simply.

"You sure?" Gus asked.

"Yup."

"Coyote?" Tank said. "Moonie can't fight a coyote!"

"None of us are a match for a coyote," Roo said quietly.

The three dogs stared across the street, hoping to see Moon Pie in the darkness. Hoping he was sitting there safely, wagging his tail, waiting for them.

A passing car slammed on the brakes. Gus spotted Lottie's neighbors Pam and Chris in the front seat.

"Quick, hide!" Gus yelled.

Roo had already started running.

"Over here!" she said, darting behind a pile of empty boxes. Gus followed her. Tank scooted in last, panting heavily.

Gus heard two car doors slam and shoes scuffing the alley pavement.

"Lottie's been worried sick about those dogs!"

"I think they ran this way."

Gus made himself as small as possible. Roo did the same.

"Where do you think they went?"

"I have no idea."

Gus slowed his breathing. He sat there as still as the birdbath in Miss Lottie's yard. Pam and Chris sounded like they were across the alley. If they took ten steps, they'd probably find him and the others.

"I don't see them."

"Well, we tried."

They walked back to their car and drove away. Gus exhaled. That had been too close. He was about to wiggle out of his hiding place when he heard a short, loud howl in the distance.

Gus looked over at Tank.

That was Moon Pie's howl.

Moon Pie

Squirming, squealing, gray shapes were falling from the trash can's lid.

RATS!

"EEEEeeeee!" Moon Pie yelped.

One rat fell on Moon Pie's head. Another fell on his back. They squealed in either terror or glee, Moon Pie couldn't tell. He yipped as their nails dug into his fur.

"Get off meeeee!!!"

Moon Pie ran and ran and ran in frantic circles. The rat on his head fell off, but the one on his back clung to him like he was riding a horse. His sharp nails pierced Moon Pie's skin.

"Get off!"

But the rat held on.

Moon Pie ran toward a rusty swing set. One of the swings hung low. If he could dash under it, maybe he'd knock the rat off.

He scampered toward it. The rat dug its claws in deeper.

The metal seat of the swing hit Moon Pie's back.

Ow!

He heard a thump. He didn't look behind him as he shot out of the yard and into the alley.

Moon Pie didn't slow down until he was sure the rat was off his back. He kept running and running until he was in another yard.

Moon Pie paused. The yard was cozy, with lots of bushes, trees, and stone statues. He glanced behind him. The rat was nowhere to be seen.

Moon Pie sat in the middle of the yard to catch his breath. He had defeated a nasty rat all by himself! *Two* nasty rats! He wished Gus or Tank had seen that!

He did not let himself think too much about what had just happened. If he did, he might not ever move from the spot he was in right at that very moment.

Moon Pie caught that bad smell coming his way again. He spun his head around but couldn't see whatever it was in the dark.

It was probably another rat! He shuddered. He did not want to see another rat again, ever.

A light went on in the house. The back door opened and

a woman stepped out. Something rustled in the bushes behind Moon Pie. He peered over his shoulder again, but couldn't see whatever it was.

"Well, if it isn't my little friend," said the woman. "I thought I heard something in the alley! It was you, cutie pie!"

Moon Pie smelled warm pudding and muffins. It was the same woman as before—the nice woman who wanted to cuddle with him.

Other good smells poured out of the nice woman's house. He could smell juicy meat and mashed potatoes and maybe even a carrot or two. Moon Pie's stomach made all kinds of growling sounds.

"Wanna come in?" she asked. She bent down and patted her thighs.

Moon Pie thought of his growling stomach and the scary smell that kept following him and the good smells coming from the woman's house. It wasn't safe outside. And inside there was good food.

He knew what he had to do.

He made his eyes big. He lifted one small paw.

The woman chuckled. "Aren't you the cutest little thing on earth! Would you like a treat?"

Moon Pie lifted his other paw. He whimpered softly.

"Awww, come here, little peanut." She reached down to scoop him up. He went limp in her arms.

"Oh no, what happened to your back?" she asked. "Let's get you inside." She hugged him close to her chest and walked inside.

It seemed like it had been forever since Moon Pie had gotten a hug. He missed it. He missed the way it smelled and the way it made him feel so, well, *melty*. So loved. He sighed.

Once inside, the woman put him carefully down on the floor of her warm kitchen. She crouched next to him and examined his back with her fingers.

"Doesn't seem too bad," she said. She went over to the sink and ran water over a towel. She bent down and rubbed the wet towel across his back. She did it softly and carefully, as if she was afraid of hurting him. It stung a little. But he was a big dog now, he could handle it. He sat quietly while she stroked his back.

"Looks okay, but we'll get you checked out tomorrow just in case." She stood and went over to the cabinets.

"I bet you'd like some steak," she said. She took out a small bowl and went over to the kitchen table. "Here," she said, cutting a piece of steak and putting it into the bowl. "How do you like this, bunny-boo?"

She put the bowl down on the floor. Moon Pie scooted over to it, wagging his tail. He gulped down the steak, then looked up and tilted his head.

"More?" she asked. She laughed and put four more

pieces in his bowl, along with a spoonful of mashed potatoes.

While he ate, the woman put down another bowl filled
with cold water. He went from food to water to food. When
he finished, he looked up at her and licked his lips.

"You were so hungry!" she said. She crouched down on
the floor and pulled him closer to her. "Let's see this tag of
yours."

She smiled as she read the tag. "Moon Pie? That's a cute
name. It says here you belong to Gertie Schneider."

He wagged his tail and barked.

"Is that who owns you? Gertie?"

Moon Pie barked again. Gertie, Gertie, Gertie!

"Okay, okay, let's call the number."

She studied the tag and repeated the phone number on
it. She stood, brought her cell out from her back pocket,
and punched the number in. She frowned and listened,
then tried punching in the number again.

"Hmmm," she said. "It's disconnected." She bit her lip
and punched in another number. "Hi, Jim, it's Nina from
next door. Listen, I found this adorable little dog in my
yard. I tried calling the number on his tag but it was disconnected. Says the name is Gertie Schneider, but there's
no address. Do you know a Gertie?"

She listened, nodding her head. She gasped softly. "Oh,
dear. That's sad. I wonder how he got here." She nodded

again. "Okay, I'll make a few more calls. Someone must know where this little guy lives now. Thanks, Jim."

After she hung up she looked down at Moon Pie. "It looks like you're stuck with me for a while until I find your human." She smiled at him. "Would you like that, honey bear?"

Moon Pie did like that. He followed her around as she washed the dishes and the pots and pans, hoping some kind of food magic would happen and another piece of steak would fall to the floor. When she was finished, he followed her into her bedroom. She turned on the TV and plopped down on her bed.

"Wanna come up, lovebug?" she asked him.

Moon Pie couldn't believe his luck. Not only was Nina a good cook and a good hugger, but her bed was even bigger than Gertie's! He barked a short, happy bark.

"Okay, but don't get too used to this. Tomorrow we're finding your human!"

She lifted him up to the bed and let him crawl under the covers. As much as he loved snuggling up close to a person again, he couldn't fall asleep right away. Something about the phone call Nina had had with the neighbor was bothering him. What did she mean when she said "that's sad"? It was such a weird thing to say.

Moon Pie stayed up a long time thinking about it.

Quinn

Quinn's hands tingled from gripping his handlebars. His voice was raspy as he called for the dogs again and again.

"Gus! Roo! Tank! Moonie!"

He rode down Miss Lottie's block, his head swiveling from one side of the street to the other. It wasn't that busy, but enough cars came by to make him nervous. Moonie was so young. He could get scared and run into the street.

"Moon Pie? Roo? Gus? Come on, you guys!"

Miss Lottie had been on the phone all day with neighbors while Quinn put up signs with the dogs' pictures. When Pam and Chris came by and said they had seen some dogs in the alley, Quinn had gotten on his bike right away to look for them again. That was over an hour ago. He had found nothing.

He wished he could take the whole afternoon back. If he hadn't looked down at his phone, maybe Gus and Tank would still be there. If he hadn't been so slow, maybe Roo wouldn't have gotten away. If, if, if.

Miss Lottie hadn't come right out and blamed him. She didn't need to. He blamed himself.

It was dark, but he pressed on. Even though they were technically Miss Lottie's dogs, Quinn loved them with everything he had. At home, Jessie ignored him and his mom always seemed too busy. It was just the opposite at Miss Lottie's. The dogs loved him. They paid attention to him.

They were his real family.

Tears welled up as he thought of them in one of the dark alleys. Tank would be breathing hard. Roo would be frantic. Gus would be hesitant, wondering where they should go next. Moon Pie would be quivering in some dark corner.

And what if they came up against a coyote, what then? He hated thinking about it.

Something stirred by a dumpster. Quinn rode over the curb and across the sidewalk. He got off his bike and walked it closer to where he had heard the sound. Resting his bike against the dumpster, he knelt down to look underneath it.

It was just a squirrel nibbling on a rice cake.

Quinn sighed. He listened for any signs of the dogs, but all he could hear were people walking on the sidewalk.

"Looking for a snack?"

Quinn looked behind him. His stomach clenched when he realized that Jessie and his friends were watching him from a few feet away. He groaned inwardly.

Not now. Please, just let me look for my dogs.

Quinn slowly stood up. He grabbed his bike with shaky hands and stood there, wondering what to do.

Jessie, Cole, and Sam moved in closer, so close Quinn could smell the fabric softener his mom used when she washed their clothes. They formed a tight circle around him.

"He just gets weirder and weirder," Cole said.

Cole was the tallest of the bunch. He also hit the hardest. Next to him stood Sam, whose white-blond hair seemed to glow in the streetlight.

"Jessie, how do you live with him?" Cole asked. "I'd move."

Quinn stared at Jessie, waiting for one of his insults.

"I'm looking for Miss Lottie's dogs. They got out," Quinn said. He didn't look at the others, just Jessie.

"Awww, you're missing your doggies," Cole said.

"How sweet," Sam said.

"I need to find them," Quinn said. He tried not to whine, but it still crept into his voice somehow. It always did. "Let me go."

Sam grabbed the handlebars and wrenched the bike out of Quinn's hands.

"'*Let me goooo!*'" Sam squealed.

"He needs to find his doggies," Cole said.

A hot flush spread across Quinn's cheeks. He could hear his heart beating in his chest.

He needed to get going. His dogs were in danger. Couldn't Jessie at least understand that? Quinn yanked his bike away from Sam so hard that Sam staggered back for a moment.

"Hey!" Sam said. "What do you think you're doing?"

Quinn pointed his bike straight at Jessie.

"I need to get by," he said.

Jessie stared back, but didn't move.

"I need to get by," Quinn said, louder. "Now."

"So?" Cole said. "What do we care?"

Quinn didn't take his eyes off Jessie. "You used to like dogs," he said. "You used to care about Murph. You loved that dog more than anyone."

Jessie's mouth twitched.

"I know you've never really forgiven me for what happened to Murph, and I'm really sorry, but you've got to let me go look for those dogs."

Quinn climbed onto the seat and jammed his left foot against the pedal. He took a deep breath.

"I don't care what you do to me tomorrow or the next day. Just let me get by so I can help them." He paused and took a deep breath. "Dad would have wanted me to find them. I just know it. He loved Murph, too."

Quinn held his breath, waiting. They didn't talk about Dad, not ever, but as soon as he mentioned him, Quinn knew that Dad was there with them somehow, in that very moment. A warm breeze gently swirled around them. Quinn felt it. He wondered if Jessie felt it, too.

Jessie's face softened. He looked into Quinn's eyes and seemed to really see him for the first time since Murph died. He nodded once and stepped aside.

Quinn didn't hesitate. He rammed his other foot onto the pedal and pumped his legs. His bike zigzagged for a second before he regained his balance.

"We're just going to let him go?" Cole asked.

Quinn sped down the street until he was almost a block away.

"Yup," Jessie said, loud enough for Quinn to hear. "Let him be."

Gus

As soon as Pam and Chris left the alley, Gus and Roo raced toward Moon Pie's howls with Tank lumbering behind them. Roo's nose guided them to pizza crusts, rat droppings, a rusted swing set, and, finally, a small brick house with a tidy yard.

Roo ran in crazy circles in the yard.

"The coyote smell, it's—"

She stopped. Her tail drooped. She backed away from something lying on the ground.

"What is it?" Gus asked. He took three quick leaps and landed next to her.

"It's—"

But Gus saw it before Roo even finished her sentence. A bloody rat lay in a heap in the grass.

Tank was standing next to him. "No way Moonie did that."

They stood there staring at the dead thing.

"We have to get Moonie home," Gus said. "Whatever got at that could easily get to him."

There was movement in the window of the house. They moved closer to it. A woman with a ponytail was opening a cabinet in the kitchen.

"He's in there," Roo said. "I know it."

They stood motionless, staring into the house.

"You're right, Roo," Gus said after a few minutes. "Watch how the woman bends down every so often. She might have her own dog, but I bet it's Moon Pie."

"What do we do?" Roo asked. She bit her tail while doing a quick spin. "What, what, WHAT?"

Tank lay down on the grass next to Gus. His panting was labored. It had been a long day. Gus knew he needed rest.

Gus, too, could feel the weariness of the day weighing him down. He hadn't had his medicine since early that morning, so his eyes felt dry and itchy. His legs ached. The hard, cold pavement in the alley had made his paws sore.

"We'll wait," Gus said. "If he's in there, and I'm pretty sure he is, he'll have to come out some time." He turned to Roo. "How close is the coyote? Is he nearby?"

Roo didn't even need to sniff. "No," she said. "But that

doesn't mean he couldn't come back."

"If he does, I'll be ready for him," Gus said. He didn't feel brave, not at all, but he made his voice sound big and bold. "If you guys want to go back, I understand. Tank, that cut looks bad. And Roo, I know this kind of thing makes you nervous."

Tank stood quickly. "Of course we'll help you," he said. "Moonie needs us, and we need Moonie. This cut is nothing."

"Yeah, Gus, we'll help, we'll help," Roo said. She pushed her nose gently against his ear.

Gus felt something loosen in his chest. Something that had been stuck. Roo was back on his side. His pack was working together again. Suddenly the aches and pains he had had just moments before melted away. He felt stronger and lighter than he had since Decker showed up.

"Thanks," he said. He nuzzled Roo back. "Let's find somewhere safe to rest."

The three of them sniffed around the yard, which was larger than most, until they found a smooth patch of dirt behind some bushes. They curled up into a warm ball of fur to stave off the chilly night air.

Gus kept staring into the yard, watching and waiting for the coyote. Every so often, he'd glance up at the woman in the kitchen window, hoping she was taking good care of Moonie.

"You know what your dog gift is?" Tank said.

Gus didn't answer. Ever since Decker had arrived, Gus had been worried that whatever his dog gift was, it wouldn't be enough to keep his pack safe.

"How much you love your pack," Tank said. He turned onto his side and heaved a long, weary sigh. "Your dog gift is love."

Gus thought about that as he kept watch. Was love the best gift for a pack leader? Wouldn't it be better for him to have a good nose, like Roo? Or strength and courage, like Tank?

Love just didn't seem like enough.

Ghost

Ghost awoke with a start. A strange moaning sound had roused him out of his sleep. When he swiveled one ear toward Miss Lottie's bedroom, he could hear faint snoring. Not a human snore. It was the new dog, Decker.

Ghost heard another moan.

"I was so *stupid*!"

It was Miss Lottie's voice, although it sounded different than it usually did. Choked. Strained. He slipped out of his underbed home and padded down the hall to the family room.

It was unsettling to see the empty dog beds and realize that the dogs were gone now. The small, excitable puppy. The big, beefy one who always smelled like mud. The three-legged one with the loud and irritating bark. And Gus, of course.

Gone.

He tried to understand why it felt so wrong. After all, they certainly bothered him with their noise, their messes, their smells. But he was used to that. Now everything felt off, as though someone had moved his bed to a different spot.

The new dog had stayed, the one that smelled of dirty water. Of all of them, he was the quietest. But he couldn't be trusted.

Ghost heard sniffling and the rustle of tissues being torn from a box. He took a few more careful steps until he found Miss Lottie in the kitchen. She sat at the table, her shoulders slumped, her head down. Crumpled balls of tissue were scattered in front of her.

"Stupid, stupid, stupid," she murmured.

Ghost was fond of Miss Lottie. She fed him and cleaned his litter box in a timely manner. She let him stay under the bed. But mostly, she never expected him to be one of those mushy, nose-rubby cats who snuggle up with their humans. That was not his style, and she knew it.

And yet, at times, he sensed that might be what she wanted. She would pat her lap and say, "Here, Ghost! Come on over for a little bit."

He never did.

He wasn't like that.

"Oh, hey, Ghostie," Miss Lottie said, smiling weakly.

"Don't suppose you want to come up?"

He gave her a slow blink, the equivalent of a cat kiss. He was never sure if she understood that.

"No, no, I don't suppose you do. I get it." She sighed and pulled out a fresh tissue to blow her nose. She made another moaning sound.

The sound shot right through to Ghost's heart. He had never seen Miss Lottie this way.

Cuddling in her lap was out of the question. What if he didn't like it? What if *she* didn't like it? She might stop feeding him and cleaning his litter box.

Or worse, she might expect it all the time. He couldn't possibly come out every day for her. That was an awful lot to ask. He had a strict schedule of fur cleaning and napping.

"Oh, Ghost. What am I going to do?" She sighed and moaned again.

He took a few steps toward her. He rose up on his hind legs and put one paw on her knee.

She looked down in surprise. "Oh!" She smiled a little. "You want to come up?"

He thought of the empty dog beds and the tissues covering the kitchen table and of his old friend Gus out in the world looking for Moon Pie.

Before he even realized it, he had leaped up into Miss Lottie's lap and accepted her scratches behind the ears.

172

He even nose-rubbed her chin.

"Thanks, Ghost," Miss Lottie said. "Thank you very, very much."

Moon Pie

"Wake up, little Moon Pie!"

Nina was already dressed. She smiled and waved a leash in front of him.

"I hope this leash is okay," she said. "It belonged to my old dog, Winnie, but I think it will work for you, too."

Moon Pie was used to leashes, but he had never really liked them. He preferred to do his business while wandering around Miss Lottie's yard. It always made him feel like an adventurer.

Tank and the others were probably in Miss Lottie's yard right this very second. Tank would be licking his belly. Roo would be running in circles. Gus would be making sure everyone was okay.

He missed them so much.

He hated that they had lied to him, hated it like he hated sneaky-pete mice, but he still thought about them all the time. Snuggling on Tank's broad back. Sleeping in the big bed. Eating popcorn. He missed it all.

"Let's go for a walk, 'kay, Tweedle-Dee-Dum?" Nina asked.

She took him off the bed, hooked him up to the leash, and walked him to the front door.

"Out we go!" she said, holding the door open.

Moon Pie stepped outside and headed to the first tree he saw. As he did his business he sniffed the breeze that sidled by him. He could smell tree bark, Nina's warm and toasty smells, a little bit of squirrel fur, which made him shudder, and . . . something else . . . something familiar . . .

TANK!

Moon Pie barked.

"TANK! TANK! TANK!"

"Moon Pie, what is it?" Nina asked. "What's wrong?"

"Tank, I smell you! Where are you! I miss you!"

"Something's bothering you," Nina said. She reached down and scooped him up. He wriggled, but she held on tight.

"Is it the leash?" Nina asked, peering into his eyes.

"TANK!"

"All right, we'll go back inside."

"But wait—Tank—"

She brought him into the house, shutting the door with her foot.

"There, there," she said. "Calm down." She gently unhooked the leash.

"Tank," Moon Pie whimpered. "I know I smelled him."

He had not realized how much he missed his Tank until Tank's special smell—kibble, grass, roots, mud, and a little bit of Tank poo—drifted by.

Loyal, trusty Tank. He had comforted Moon Pie after his first bath at Miss Lottie's. He had calmed him when a squirrel teased him. He had made sure that Moon Pie was always warm and safe. Moon Pie should have known that Tank would find him.

Moon Pie had also smelled other familiar scents. Roo's worry had a certain bitterness to it, and Gus took a medicine that made him smell sharp and tangy, like cheese. All those smells had come forward, too.

They were out there, and they were looking for him!

But then Moon Pie remembered.

They had lied.

All of them.

Gertie, sweet old Gertie, was searching for him, and they had not told him about it. They had let him believe she was just on vacation and that she'd be picking him up soon. They had kept him from the person he loved most in the world.

He hung his head and stared at the floor. They could sit out there as long as they wanted to. He was never, ever going to join them!

"Want some breakfast, pumpkin bunny?" Nina asked. "I'm making bacon."

Moon Pie's head snapped up. Why think of those old dogs when he had bacon to eat? He trotted over to Nina's feet and planted himself in front of her while she cooked all kinds of delicious things.

"Here you go," she said. She bent down with a plate full of eggs, toast, and bacon. He sniffed hard, concentrating on the wonderful smells.

"We're going for a little ride today," Nina said. She gathered her keys and her purse as she spoke to him. "We need to get those scratches checked out."

After she was finished eating, she scooped him up. "I don't think you liked that leash, so I'll just carry you."

She carried him out the door and into the backyard. Moon Pie smelled Tank, Gus, and Roo even more strongly now. He peered over Nina's shoulder and saw them crouched behind some bushes.

He looked right into Tank's eyes for a long moment. Tank seemed to be pleading with him to come back.

Moon Pie turned away and gave Nina a lick on the cheek. He hoped they all saw it.

Tank

Tank squeezed his eyes shut.

Moon Pie, *his Moon Pie*, had known they were there, and yet he had turned away from them. From him.

Tank felt a paw gently nudge his side.

"We can find him," Gus said. "But we should leave now. Get up."

Tank didn't feel like getting up. He didn't feel like going after Moon Pie. He didn't feel like doing anything at all. He had failed miserably. He hadn't been a good guardian to Moon Pie. If he had, Moon Pie wouldn't have left.

"I'm staying here," Tank said. He squeezed his eyes shut tighter and burrowed his head into his paws. He felt as heavy as a bag of rocks.

"Come on, Tank," Gus said. "We have to see him face to face and explain."

Tank sighed, but didn't budge.

"Here, eat this. It'll give you energy."

Tank opened his eyes. Gus had dropped an especially ripe-smelling piece of bologna right near his nose. Tank sniffed it, licked it, and sighed. "He saw us and he just looked away." He put his head on his paws. "He's mad. He'll never forgive us."

"That's why we have to tell him what really happened," Gus said. "We'll have to tell him that we lied because . . . because . . . we thought it was best for him."

"We should have told him the truth," Tank said. "He has every reason to be mad at us. He risked his life because we didn't tell him about Gertie."

Even though Tank had agreed to lie about Gertie, he knew now that his sweet little Moon Pie was tougher than he'd thought.

Maybe he had been overprotective. Maybe it was okay for others to get hurt every once in a while.

"We'll tell him we made a mistake," Gus said. "We'll explain why we did it. I don't think he'll stay mad. He's not that kind of dog." He looked at Tank. "But we have to try, Tank."

Gus was right. They had to tell Moon Pie why they'd done it. Moon Pie needed to hear their side of the story.

Tank stood.

"Okay," he said. "I'm ready." He slurped up the bologna in one gulp.

Roo sniffed the air. "We have to leave SOON," she said. "If he goes too far in that car, I'll never be able to pick up his scent!"

She started running in quick, urgent circles around the yard. "And I smell coyote, Gus! It's back!"

"I smell him, too," Gus said. "He's probably hunting for food. Let's go."

Tank gave himself a gentle shake. He winced. The gash on his side had spilt open. He reached over and tried to lick it, but he was too big.

Gus moved closer to him and gently licked the wound.

"It's deep," Gus said. "And I don't like the way it smells. We need to get you back to Miss Lottie's so she can take you to the vet."

"I'm fine," Tank said. The scrape stung, but it was bearable. He slowly walked out into the yard. "Come on, Roo, which way do we go?"

Roo sat. She stayed very still as she pointed her nose to the sky. She looked right, then left.

"This way," she said.

Moon Pie

Nina opened the window on Moon Pie's side of the car.

"Thought you might like a little fresh air and sunshine, snugglebug," she said.

Moon Pie stood on the seat so he could stick his head out the window. He loved the way the air pushed against his fur and how all the smells in the world rushed toward him. He sniffed hard as they zoomed down the street, hoping to get a whiff of Gertie. They drove past two women on bikes, a mail carrier, and a girl on a skateboard. When he saw a big shaggy dog being pulled down the sidewalk by his human, he called out to him with the customary dog greeting.

"Happy peeing!"

"Thanks!" said the other dog, whose human was impatiently tugging on his leash. "Good peeing to you, too!"

Nina reached over and stroked Moon Pie's back. "You'll love Dr. Happ," she said. "She's very gentle."

Moon Pie stopped wagging his tail, and his ears perked up. Gertie took him to a Dr. Happ.

He stared outside at the people and homes rushing by. Maybe there were lots of Dr. Happs. Maybe all vets were called Dr. Happ.

But when they passed a small house with a stone statue of a large frog out front, Moon Pie let out a sharp bark. Weeds covered the yard. A broken stroller was parked by the front steps.

Moon Pie's heart beat wildly. He knew that frog! He knew those weeds! He knew that stroller!

He knew that house!

When he and Gertie went on walks, they passed it, and when they did, Gertie would always say, "That house sure does need some love and paint."

The house was only a little bit away from Gertie's house!

He scratched at the door frantically.

"Gertie! Gertie! I'm coming, I'm coming!"

"Sweetpea, what's the matter?" Nina asked. She pulled the car into a parking lot. "Are you afraid of the vet? Is that it?"

He recognized the building in front of them. This was where they saw Dr. Happ! Gertie lived right nearby!

Nina reached over to grab him, but he wiggled away.

"I'm coming, Gertie!"

Nina shook her head as she got out of the car. She opened the door on Moon Pie's side, but before she could grab him, he jumped down and raced toward the sidewalk.

"Moon Pie, stop!"

But Moon Pie didn't stop. Finally, finally, he knew where he was going!

He could hear Nina calling as he ran.

"Moon Pie, stop! NO!"

The big shaggy dog barked his approval. "Go, little dude! Find your freedom!"

Moon Pie looked to his left and saw an alley. He dashed over to it.

He raced halfway down the length of the alley and stopped.

There was the garage.

Gertie's garage!

The door on the side was open, just like it always was. Moon Pie darted inside to hide from Nina.

His heart felt all fluttery just being in the old garage again. He did a quick spin. He was in Gertie's garage! He had made it there all by himself!

He knew the garage well. He and Gertie would climb into the old car that lived there, the car with the scratched leather seats. Gertie would say, "We're off on an adventure!" every time, even if they were just going to the post office.

It was dark inside, so dark he couldn't see, but he could smell strange scents wafting about. What puzzled him was that he couldn't smell the scratched leather seats or the mulch or Gertie's gardening gloves. Instead he smelled bleach and cardboard boxes. They were not Gertie smells.

And the car that was in there wasn't Gertie's car.

He could still hear Nina calling his name, but she was moving farther and farther away. It was probably best. Now that he was finally back at Gertie's, he didn't need Nina's bacon anymore. He would need to keep quiet, though. If Nina found him, she'd try to bring him back to her house.

Once he was sure Nina was gone, he crept out of the garage. His heart thumped as he trotted closer to the house. He smelled oak leaves, the warmth of the brick, the neighbor's cat.

But there were so many new smells, smells that didn't go with Gertie. Fresh paint. Glass cleaner.

Something wasn't right.

Three tidy towers of cardboard boxes sat on the back deck.

He stared into the kitchen window, hoping to see Gertie in her polka-dotted robe watering her plants.

Gertie's nasty, nasty sister was still there. She was reaching up into the cupboards and putting dishes into a box on the counter.

She must have dropped Gertie off after their vacation. But why hadn't she left yet? Where was Gertie?

He waited and waited for Gertie to come into view. She was probably cooking something for her sister. Maybe her beef stew, or her lasagna.

He preferred the beef stew, but the lasagna was pretty good, too.

He started to bark and then stopped. Gertie's nasty, nasty sister would put him in the basement again. He'd wait until she left, then he would bark at the back door. Gertie would pick him up and swing him through the air, just like she used to.

He crept over to his favorite hiding spot, the thick bushes he hid behind when he didn't feel like coming in when Gertie called him.

The back door opened. Gertie's sister grunted as she placed another box on the deck. She reached into her pocket, took out a tissue, and dabbed at her eyes. She sighed.

Moon Pie wondered if maybe she had a cold, but then a soft, tired smell drifted toward him. It smelled like an old, frayed rope.

She was *sad*. Moon Pie could smell it coming off her in waves. It was the same smell Gertie had when she watched movies where people died.

Why was Gertie's sister so sad? And what were all those boxes for?

Then Moon Pie remembered something else. Miss Lottie had had that same sad smell when she had walked with him to her house for the very first time. Oh, sure, it was mixed in with popcorn and dog smells, but it had been there, and Moon Pie had ignored it.

Moon Pie tucked himself into a tight ball and watched as Gertie's sister came outside onto the deck. She picked up a box and walked across the yard to the garage. He could hear the beep of a car door being unlocked. Moments later, she came back into the yard and brought another box from the deck to the car. When all the boxes on the back deck were gone, she pulled the car out of the garage and drove away.

The sun sat low in the gray sky. Moon Pie shivered. He had waited all day for Gertie, but she never came out. He hadn't seen her through the window, making lunch or reading the paper. He hadn't seen her in the yard, breathing in the fresh air or looking up at the clouds.

He hadn't seen her, or smelled her, at all.

Gus

The pack was moving slowly. Gus hadn't had his medicine since he left Miss Lottie's the day before. The deep aches and pains in his legs had gotten worse, and his eyes were crusty and dry. The three dogs ate scraps of food from garbage cans they tipped over, but it wasn't enough. They had to stop a few times so Tank could rest.

The faint smell of coyote had wafted in and out as they traveled. It wore on Gus's nerves.

"I think Moonie is this way," Roo said as she trotted over to an old chair that had been dumped in the alley. Roo had lost the scent, found the scent, then lost it again.

"This is taking forever," Tank said. "Be honest. You can't find the scent, can you?"

Roo growled. "I'm trying my best, okay? I AM TRYING MY BEST."

Tank growled back at her. "Well, it's not good enough!"

"Stop it, you two," Gus said. "This isn't helping."

Roo sniffed at the old chair. "Someone else has marked this besides Moon Pie. I smell a big male with too many treats in his diet." She looked to her right, then her left. "Like him."

Gus turned to see who Roo was looking at. In a nearby yard, a large, shaggy dog was sprawled on the grass, gnawing on a Frisbee.

"Maybe he knows something," Gus said. Wincing at the pain, he got up slowly and made his way over to the big dog.

"Hey," Gus said, speaking through the fence. "Nice Frisbee."

"It's mine," the dog said without looking up.

"I don't want it," Gus said.

The shaggy dog stopped gnawing and stared at Gus. "Why not? It's a good Frisbee."

He seemed annoyed. This was not what Gus wanted.

"I'm not here to play—" Gus started.

"That's good, 'cause I don't want to share my Frisbee."

"I know, I know, don't worry!" Gus said, exasperated. "I'm looking for a dog. I'm wondering if you've seen him."

"There are a lot of dogs around, dude."

"This dog is a small pug, practically a puppy. He's probably with a woman with a ponytail."

Tank and Roo were now standing next to Gus.

The shaggy dog stopped gnawing. He stood and puffed out his chest. "Who are you guys?"

"No need to go all alpha on us," Roo said. "We're just looking for our friend Moon Pie."

The dog flopped back down. "Moon Pie is kind of a dumb name."

"We didn't name him," Gus said. He glanced at Tank and Roo. "Come on, this is a waste of time." He turned to leave.

"I saw that little dude," the shaggy dog said.

Gus stopped.

"Where?" he asked.

"He was running like a crazy squirrel! Running, running, running like his life depended on it. Some lady was calling after him, but he didn't care."

"Okay, but where?" Tank asked.

The shaggy dog got up, shook his head, and dipped down into a long stretch. "Looked like he was running away from the vet. Can't say I blame him. It's two blocks that way." He nodded his head to his right. "You can smell the fear from here. He was heading down Saunders Street, away from the vet's office. Smart dog."

Roo lifted her head. "I smell the vet's office. I do I do I do! If we want to find Moonie we need to go this way!" she said.

She loped along down the alley away from the vet's office, with Gus and Tank doing their best to keep up with her.

"I smell him I smell him I smell him," she sang.

"I . . . hope . . . she's . . . right . . . ," Tank said, huffing beside Gus.

Roo stopped. Her right ear shot straight up. Her body quivered.

"We're close," she said quietly.

"Be very quiet," Gus said. "If he knows we're following him, he'll hide."

They peered into a yard with swings and another yard with a patio. Nothing. The sun was low in the sky. None of them could see that well in the dark. If they didn't find Moon Pie soon, they'd have to stop and find somewhere to sleep for the night.

Then, as they were passing a garage, all three caught it.

Moon Pie's scent. Moon Pie's frightened, sad scent.

The three dogs trotted into the yard next to the garage. They looked everywhere. Finally, Gus found him behind some bushes, huddled in a corner, staring at the house.

"He's here," Gus said.

Roo galloped over to Gus with Tank chugging along behind her. They stood in front of the small dog, waiting for him to acknowledge them, but Moon Pie just kept staring at the house.

"Moonie?" Gus said. He took a step toward him.

"She's not there," Moon Pie said.

"No, she's not," Tank said.

"I think she died," Moon Pie said quietly. "I think that's why her nasty, nasty sister is so sad. She's packing Gertie's stuff into boxes because Gertie died."

Gus and Tank exchanged looks.

"Yes," Tank said. "I'm so sorry, Moonie."

Moon Pie blinked a long, slow blink. "I'll never see her again. I'll never get to say goodbye."

"I know it's hard, Moonie," Gus said. "We should have told you the truth. It was wrong to keep it from you."

They all sat in silence, staring at the house.

"I heard her, you know," Moon Pie said.

Gus tilted his head, waiting.

"I was crossing the street and I shouldn't have been and I wasn't going fast enough and she said, 'Run, Moon Pie, run!' It was like she was right there next to me."

He looked into their faces. "She was there, I know she was, and no one can ever say any different."

"I believe you," Roo said.

"So do I," Tank said.

"The humans who really and truly loved us are with us all the time," Gus said. "Like Miss Lottie. She misses you, Moonie."

"I miss her lots, too," Moon Pie said softly. He looked down at the ground and sighed.

They walked back home in the dimming afternoon light. Roo in front. Gus and Moon Pie behind her. Tank lagging behind.

Dry leaves skittered across their path. A crow cawed off in the distance. For a moment, Gus thought he caught the coyote's scent again, swirling around in the cold November wind.

"You know what else I've missed?" Moon Pie asked.

"What?" Gus asked.

"Miss Lottie's popcorn. Hers is the best."

"I'm sure that when you get home, you can have as much as you want," Gus said.

"Is Decker still there?" Moon Pie asked.

"Yes," Gus said.

"Oh."

"Moonie, don't you worry about Decker," Tank said. "We'll have you back in the big bed in no time, just wait and see."

There was a strange determination in Tank's voice. He would be hankering for a fight once they got home.

Gus's head filled with concern. He would probably have to make a lot of quick decisions, and quick decisions were not his strength.

He really wished he had a tennis ball to gnaw on.

Decker

Decker woke up with a start. His breathing was ragged. His blood thrummed through his veins.

They were coming back. All of them.

He could feel it. There was a certain knowing in the pads of his feet and at the end of his tail. They were on their way, and they were determined to change things back to the way they had been.

Well, that was not going to happen. Things were finally as they should be. He had Miss Lottie and the house and the bed and the treats all to himself. Everything was perfect.

Miss Lottie snored and turned onto her back. Tomorrow she would be thrilled. Ecstatic. She might even let the putrid little pug back into the big bed.

He needed sleep. Tomorrow he would be ready.

Decker Before

He was born in a box by a dumpster.

Cold. Dark.

Rough hands hoisted him out of the box.

Rough hands spanked him hard when he peed on the floor, then shoved him down into the cold, dark basement.

Rough hands pulled, pushed, yanked, tugged, smacked.

Long days turned into long months of living in the dark basement.

Those same rough hands put him in a box and brought him to town in the middle of the night. A new puppy, a pug puppy, had arrived, and he was no longer needed or wanted.

He lived on the streets, fought on the streets, until he was caught and put in a cage. He had food, and he had water, but the cage was cold and dark.

Too cold. Too dark.

He bit the cage until his mouth bled, then bit it again.

He stayed there for months.

Then came the gentle hands, the kind voice. Gray, frizzy hair.

And even though she took him out of the cold and the dark, he was still haunted by them. He couldn't shake the feeling that the cold and the dark had taken root deep inside him, and that because of this, he could never, ever know love.

He felt broken. Like something inside him had withered and died.

Decker knew one thing for sure. No one wants a broken dog.

Quinn

Quinn couldn't sleep. His thoughts were a jumbled mess of fear and worry. He thought briefly of Jessie and the others, but for once, they weren't his biggest concern. For the first time since their bullying started, he thought that maybe, *maybe* it had all come to an end. He wasn't sure, but it felt like something had shifted when he stood up to them. As though they were seeing him as a real person for the first time.

And Jessie. Letting him go like that. Quinn hoped that he had somehow remembered that they were still brothers. Brothers who had once hung out together, who had built forts together. Brothers who shared the same dad.

But his dogs were out there all alone. After hours and hours of looking, he still hadn't found them.

He got up to get a drink of water. As soon as his feet touched the cold bathroom tile floor, he stopped. The hairs on his arms prickled. He held on to the door frame and closed his eyes.

A warm, calm feeling settled over him. He knew with a strange certainty that they were coming back. All of them. They were worn out, shivering. And they were waiting for him to open the gate.

Quinn shoved his feet into his sneakers, pulled on a heavy sweatshirt, and tiptoed down the hall. His mother's room was quiet. Jessie's bedroom door was open a crack.

Quinn crept down the stairs. A light was on in the kitchen. Quinn peered into the room and saw Jessie standing by the refrigerator, taking out a milk carton. He turned and started when he saw Quinn, then quickly composed himself.

Jessie raised his eyebrows. "Where are you going?" he asked.

"The dogs," Quinn said. "They're back."

Jessie poured the milk into a glass, sipped it, then set it back down.

"How do you know?"

Quinn shrugged.

Jessie paused. "Better hurry," he said. He walked over to the hooks by the back door, grabbed their dad's old wool hat, and tossed it to Quinn. "It's cold out."

Quinn pulled the hat over his ears.

"Thanks," he said.

He wanted to say more, but wasn't sure what. He didn't know how to act with Jessie now, but he hoped, in time, he would. He gave him a quick nod as he slipped out the back door and into the night air.

Quinn unlocked his bike and rolled it out of the garage. Sliding onto the worn seat, he blew on his hands and then grabbed the handlebars and headed to Miss Lottie's.

Gus

As much as they all wanted to rest, Gus pushed them on through the night. They were tired and hungry, but he knew Miss Lottie would have taken their escape hard. Prolonging their return was unfair. She needed to have them safe and back where they belonged, and where they belonged was with her.

And the coyote, Gus knew, was never very far from them. It seemed to be moving with the pack. Gus scanned the bushes, hoping to see the glow of its eyes, but the coyote kept itself hidden.

Roo felt the coyote, too. She and Gus exchanged a few worried glances when the smell of it was particularly strong.

When Gus wasn't worrying about the coyote, he was

worrying about Decker. He was an unpredictable dog, and that concerned Gus. It was hard to plan a strategy if he didn't know how Decker would react.

"You know, Gus, Decker is sleeping in your bed during the day, and he's sleeping in Miss Lottie's bed at night," Roo told him.

Gus bristled at the idea of Decker in his bed. The bed Miss Lottie had sewn just for him. The bed that smelled like his favorite tennis balls. The bed he had slept in ever since he arrived at Miss Lottie's years ago.

"He says he's in charge now," Roo continued. She eyed Gus nervously as they trotted down the alley in the moonlight.

"Well, he's not," Gus snapped.

"I feel like maybe I had something to do with that," Roo said. "The way I followed him around and all. But then he started acting weird and mean. Ugh!" She shuddered. "You would never act that way, Gus. You're always so sweet and kind." She gently rubbed her nose against his. "You're a true pack leader. Not him."

Gus felt like his heart might burst "Thanks, Roo," he said quietly.

They all kept going, Tank grunting with each step, Roo raising her ears or twitching her nose every so often.

"I can't wait to take a long nap in my bed, that's for sure," Tank said.

"Me, too," Gus said.

Roo stopped walking. She stood in the middle of the alley, quivering.

"Roo? What's wrong?" Gus said.

But then he smelled it. Coyote.

"Don't move," Roo said.

They stood, ears trembling, noses in the air.

The coyote was close, all right. One house away, maybe two.

"Hey," Gus said. "Where's Moonie?"

"I don't know," Roo said. She sniffed the air.

Gus's heart beat faster. "Moonie? Come on, now. No playing," he said.

Tank raced ahead of them on his short, stubby legs. "Moonie, where are you?" he yelled. He stopped and frantically looked from one side of the alley to the other.

Gus scanned the bushes at the edge of the alley. If Moonie was there, he was doing a good job of hiding.

"Moonie!" Tank called. He ran down the alley faster than Gus had ever seen him run. "Come back!"

"Tank, wait, no!" Roo said.

And then they all heard it. A growl so fierce and menacing, it sent a cold wave of fear down Gus's back.

"Tank! Help me!" yelled Moon Pie.

Tank spun around and raced toward Moon Pie's voice.

"Tank, stop! Be careful!" Gus yelled. He sprinted after Tank, with Roo at his side.

They backtracked until they came to a garage with a

line of trash cans along the side of it. One of them had tipped over. Half a burger and some fries were sprawled across the papers and empty cans. Moon Pie was cowering against the garage. Standing between him and the burger was the coyote.

"Help, please, help!" Moon Pie cried.

Gus froze. His mouth went dry. Every hair on his body tingled.

The coyote had matted fur and long teeth. It growled at them as they edged closer.

Moon Pie whimpered. "I was so hungry and I stopped to eat this burger and then he was here! Help!"

"It's okay," Gus said quietly. "We won't let anything happen to you."

But coyotes were fast and vicious. Gus's pack was tired and hurt. If the coyote attacked, Gus worried they wouldn't be able to defend themselves.

"I'm afraid," Moon Pie said.

"Stay calm, Moonie," Gus said. "We're here now." He tried to make his voice sound firm, but it came out wobbly.

The coyote pinned its ears back and snarled at Moon Pie.

Tank growled. A loud, angry growl. He took two steps toward the coyote.

"Tank . . . ," Gus warned.

"He's not going to hurt my Moonie!" Tank said. He barked a few sharp barks and pawed at the ground as if he were about to charge. "Besides, there's only one of him!"

Tank snapped his jaws. Spittle flew across the pavement.

The air changed.

The sharp, dangerous scent of the coyote was still there. Still dark and heavy.

But there was something else, too. Something beneath the cold, watery scent.

Fear.

Gus took a slow, tentative step toward the coyote. He could see the wild creature's ribs. He smelled its hunger and its pain.

But mostly he smelled its fear.

The coyote looked at Gus with pale, frightened eyes. Its tail dipped down low. It was really just a pup. A pup without a pack.

And Gus knew.

He knew with his deep-down dogginess that this coyote was alone, and it was hungry, and it was just trying to survive in the only way it knew how.

"Let him be, Tank," Gus said.

"What? No!" Tank said.

"He's hungry," Gus said, without taking his eyes off the coyote. "And he doesn't have a pack. That's why he's been following us. He needs the food we've been finding." Gus nodded to the coyote. "Go ahead," he said. "Eat it all. We'll find something else."

Tank grunted. He backed away and stood next to Gus. "All right," he said. "I guess it's okay."

Moon Pie carefully crept around the coyote and stood next to Tank.

"It's the right thing to do," Roo said quietly. "Gus always knows the right thing to do."

The coyote paused, then wolfed down the burger. It glanced up at Gus once, then went back to eating.

"Come on," Gus said to his pack. "Let's go home."

Dealing with Decker, who was, by now, well rested and well fed, would be a lot tougher than dealing with this weak and sickly coyote.

There would be a confrontation. Decker was slyer than Gus, and bolder. He didn't care about consequences, and this bothered Gus more than anything. Decker had no compassion and didn't obey the rules. He would bite, rip, tear. He would do whatever he could to keep them out.

Gus had to be bigger than that. He had to be smarter. He just hoped his deep-down dogginess would show him how.

Gus

Just as Gus had expected. Roo found a promising garbage pail.

"Lots of goodies inside this one," she said. She had her front paws on the can and was sniffing at the lid. "Come on, help me out," she said to them.

They all put their front paws on it. One big shove sent it clattering to the ground. Greasy, gooey tidbits spilled out— onion rings, fried chicken, coleslaw, macaroni and cheese, Jell-O, poundcake, as well as a few other things they weren't quite sure of. They gobbled it down within minutes.

"That was fun!" Moon Pie said. "We're just like that wild coyote!"

"Well, not quite," Gus said, thinking of the way the lone coyote's ribs poked out of its fur.

The journey home was easier after their feast. Soon they were only a block away from Miss Lottie's.

"So what's our plan, Gus?" asked Tank.

Gus kept walking, thoughts swirling around in his brain. He didn't believe in fighting. He believed in the power of the pack, and that all dogs could find peace if they could see how important they were to the pack. Roo, with her amazing speed and sniffing abilities. Tank's fierceness and loyalty. Moon Pie's charm. They all had their gifts, each and every one of them.

If that was so, if every dog had a gift, what was Decker's? There didn't seem to be any goodness in him at all.

And yet, in a strange way, Decker had made the pack stronger. More unified. And more honest. They probably never would have told Moon Pie about Gertie if Decker hadn't forced them to. Maybe bringing the pack together was Decker's strange gift.

"Well?" Tank asked.

Miss Lottie's fence was in full view now. Gus saw the hole they had all escaped through and the gate Quinn was always careful to close and the garden rake that had lain in the grass all fall.

"We don't fight," Gus said.

"Gus—" Tank began.

"No, Tank," Gus said firmly. "There will be another way. There always is."

Instead of crawling through the tight hole that had scratched Tank so badly, they decided to wait by the fence. Gus knew the coyote wouldn't be bothering them now. The sun would be up in a few hours, and then Miss Lottie would be bringing Decker out for his morning time in the yard.

The wind howled through the trees. Gus shivered. He felt a deep ache in his bones. He tried to rest, but it was too cold.

Tank wandered over and plunked down next to him. Roo and Moon Pie followed. They snuggled in close. Gus smelled their fur and their warm breath. He sighed and let his eyes close. They would need all their strength for whatever was ahead.

Quinn

The alley was silent, except for the sound of the wind in the trees and Quinn's wheels skidding across the pavement.

Maybe there was nothing to be excited about. Maybe the strange feeling he had had in the bathroom about the four dogs returning home was just that—a strange feeling, nothing more.

Quinn pedaled faster, thinking of what would happen if Gus and the others returned. Ever since the new dog had arrived, things had changed, and Miss Lottie didn't seem to understand. Maybe Decker did look like her sweet Mr. Beans, but Decker's eyes told another story.

Quinn knew that all dogs were different, like people. Some were touchy, which could make them nippy. Others were mistrusting. Some had led tough lives and were wary of new humans or new dogs.

Quinn understood this. It was why he was so good with them. He knew all about the loss of trust, and how someone who was supposed to be your family could turn out to be your worst enemy.

But now he also knew that all that could change, and like his dad's old wool hat hanging on a hook, hope and love were never far away.

The cold night air bit his face and his hands, but he couldn't go back. He kept pedaling until he saw them, just as he knew he would.

They were curled up in a big ball of fur. Quinn walked his bike up behind them. They all jumped at the sound of tires on the cement.

"You're back," Quinn said quietly. His heart swelled as relief poured over him.

They were safe. His family was safe.

They raced over to him on stiff and wobbly legs. They wiggled their bodies and wagged their tails wildly while taking turns jumping on him.

"Moon Pie, we were so worried!" Quinn said, his voice trembling. He lay his bike down and sat on the ground, pulling Moon Pie into his lap.

The other dogs climbed all over him, nudging his cheeks with their cold, wet noses and pawing at his legs and arms.

Tears rolled down Quinn's face. Gus licked them off. "You're back, you're really back," Quinn whispered.

He wiped his face with his sleeve, then got up, leaned his bike against the fence, and led them through the gate.

Early morning sunlight filled the yard and lit up the dogs' coats. The whole scene—wiggling dogs and sunny yard—belonged in a scrapbook.

He never wanted to forget this moment.

"Miss Lottie is going to be so happy," he said. He rapped on the door loudly. He heard footsteps and the door being unlocked, and then it swung open.

"Oh my goodness!" Miss Lottie cried.

She paused a moment, hands clasped to her chest, before crouching down and accepting the dogs into her arms. She muttered "oh my goodness" over and over as tears streamed down her cheeks.

Quinn stared at his feet. He was afraid he might cry in front of Miss Lottie. He hadn't cried in front of anyone for a long time. Crying, he found, had always made things worse.

"This never would have happened if I had fixed the fence," he said quietly. "Or if I had been paying attention when they were out in the yard. I should have . . . I don't know . . . been better . . . helped more . . ."

He couldn't finish. His throat was tight with tears.

Miss Lottie stood. She gave him a big smile, then pulled him into her warm, squishy body for a hug.

"It's okay," she said quietly, rocking him gently. "It's all going to be okay."

Roo

As soon as Roo entered the house, she paused, her body tense, her tail stiff. Where was Decker? She couldn't see him, but she could smell Decker's anger wafting from Miss Lottie's bedroom. She wondered if he would be angriest at her. After all, she had gone along with his leadership for a little while. She had been his sidekick. And everyone knew she was the best at tracking smells. He would probably blame her for bringing them all back.

Roo felt the urge to MOVE. She started to spin.

"Roo, shhh, it's okay," Quinn said. He bent down and held her around her waist to keep her from spinning.

Roo caught her breath. She gave Quinn a quick lick on the cheek before he stood.

"How did you know they were there?" Miss Lottie asked Quinn. She took an apple out of the fridge and handed it to him.

Quinn bit into the apple. "I just sort of felt it, I guess."

Miss Lottie frowned and nodded. "Funny. I got up to get some water and decided to look out in the yard. I'm not sure why." She shook her head and laughed. "And there you were! With them! Incredible!"

After lots more hugging, Miss Lottie poured heaps of dried kibble into bowls for each dog, mixed in with some wet food, and refilled their water bowls. She plopped an especially large treat into each bowl.

"There!" she said. "Have at it!"

Roo and the others raced to the bowls, bent their heads down, and got to work. Their slurping noises filled the kitchen.

"There he is!" cried Miss Lottie. "How about this, eh, Decker? Your pals are back!"

Roo stopped eating. She turned to see Decker in the kitchen doorway, glaring.

"What are you doing here?" Tank asked. "Don't you know you don't belong?"

"Quiet, Tank," Gus warned.

Decker sat. He licked his paw. "Oh, I belong here, all right. You're the ones who don't belong."

Roo choked on her food.

"Oh, Roo, honey, slow down!" Miss Lottie said. She knelt down and stroked Roo's fur until Roo stopped coughing. "You're safe now. Everything's okay."

Roo wished she could be that sure.

Gus

After cleaning Tank's and Moon Pie's scratches, Miss Lottie spread a thick and smelly ointment on them. Quinn fixed the hole in the fence, but Gus wasn't worried about any of them escaping again. It was Decker he was worried about. When the dogs were out in the yard, he kept Decker within his field of vision at all times. If Decker got up to move, Gus moved with him, making sure he was only a few feet away.

Decker barely seemed to notice. He looked calm, as if nothing in the world could bother him. But Gus knew that something *must* bother him; otherwise, he wouldn't act the way he did. Dogs like Decker had deep wounds. It was only a matter of finding out where they were.

The day wore on. Gus grew wearier and wearier. By

the time Miss Lottie started turning out the lights, he was splayed out on his bed.

"Moon Pie, you've been through a lot, you little sweetie," Miss Lottie said, swooping the small dog into her arms. "I'm sure Decker won't mind sleeping out here tonight, will you, Decker? I haven't made a bed for you yet, but this couch should do for now."

Miss Lottie patted the old plaid couch in the family room. Decker simply stared at Moon Pie in Miss Lottie's arms.

"It's only eight thirty, but I'm beat," Miss Lottie said. "Good night, kiddos." She blew them all a kiss before turning out the last light.

As soon as the lights were off, Roo got up from her bed and snuggled in next to Tank on his big bed.

Gus heard Decker walk over to the couch and hop up onto it. Maybe he was tired, too. It had been a tense day for all of them.

When he heard Decker snoring, Gus let out a sigh of relief. They had made it through the day without a fight. He rested his head on his paws and fell into an uneasy sleep.

Moon Pie

Moon Pie squirmed in Miss Lottie's arms.

"Okay, okay," Miss Lottie said, laughing. She put Moon Pie down in the middle of the bed. "Happy now?"

Moon Pie barked one sharp bark, stuck his butt in the air, then scooted around the bed in small circles.

"What a silly little boy!" Miss Lottie said. "It's only a bed!"

Oh, but Miss Lottie's bed was so much more! It was soft and bouncy, and the blankets weren't too thick or too thin. Good smells were smeared all over it, spread thick like peanut butter on bread. Moon Pie detected popcorn and butter and salt and salami. He rolled on his back, rubbing the smells into his fur.

Then there were the smells of Miss Lottie herself, her

skin, her hair, the dirt and grass of her yard, all the soapy, sweaty goodness that made her unique.

And was that ham? With mayo? Moon Pie dug his face into her pillow to get a better sniff.

But then there were the Decker smells, too, smells that made Moon Pie pause. Decker had a cold, watery smell. Moon Pie hoped Miss Lottie would be washing his smell out soon.

Miss Lottie sat down on the bed and patted a space beside her. "Come here, little one! I missed you!"

Moon Pie hopped over a pillow and landed on Miss Lottie's lap.

Miss Lottie had tears in her eyes as she stroked Moon Pie's ears. "I didn't think I'd ever see you again. I missed you so much." She picked him up and held him in her arms before putting him back down on the bed. "Don't play any more silly tricks like that, okay?"

She got up and headed into the bathroom. Soon Moon Pie heard the water running. The sounds of Miss Lottie gargling made Moon Pie sigh. He was home. Home home home. He closed his eyes and dug his nose into the pillow. He had missed this. Even though it was exciting being out on his own with the rats and the pizza and the coyote, he had missed this cozy bed with its warm smells.

And he had missed Miss Lottie, who loved him from the tip of his tail to the tip of his nose.

The faint sound of paws on carpet startled Moon Pie. He pricked up his ears and opened his eyes.

There, next to Miss Lottie's bed, was Decker. His front paws were on the mattress. He was looking at Moon Pie with hungry eyes.

"Get out," Decker said.

Moon Pie's heart beat so fast, he worried it might explode. He got up with shaky legs and stared at Decker's long, lean face with its cool, pale eyes.

"Miss Lottie said I was allowed to sleep on the big bed tonight."

Decker cocked his head to one side. "But Moon Pie, don't you remember? You're the lowest member of the pack. You do what I say."

Moon Pie didn't respond

"I said, *you do what I say.*"

"Miss Lottie said . . ."

"Miss Lottie is not the boss here anymore."

Moon Pie trembled. He whimpered softly.

He did not like that idea one bit.

Gus

Gus opened his eyes and shook his head. He had fallen asleep too hard and too fast. He looked over at the couch, where Decker was sleeping.

Empty!

Gus sprang up. He held himself still, straining to listen for any sounds of the big dog.

But he didn't need to hear him. He knew exactly where Decker was. Gus raced down the hall. He stood in the doorway of Miss Lottie's room, letting his eyes adjust to the dark.

"I'm coming up there whether you—" Decker began.

"Stop," said Gus.

Moon Pie and Decker turned toward him.

Gus stood in the doorway, his fur on end, his tail stiff

and standing straight up.

"You don't have to get off the bed, Moonie," he said.

Decker sighed. "I am so tired of you, Gus."

"I bet you are," Gus said. "Tell me, what is it about the bed that you want so much? Because I don't think it's the smells. I think it's . . . something else." Gus sniffed the air.

"Really? What is it, then?" Decker asked.

Gus paused for a long time. He sniffed hard. There was something about Decker's smell. Something different than his usual hard, watery smell. Something familiar, too.

The coyote. Decker smelled the same as the coyote.

Finally it dawned on Gus. Decker, prowling around at night, always wanting to be on the big bed near Miss Lottie. He knew what Decker's wound was.

"You're afraid of the dark."

Without any warning growl, Decker sprang toward him. He stopped in front of Gus, teeth bared.

Gus stood still, very still, even when Decker leaned in close, snapping his jaws.

"Don't do this," Gus said.

Decker growled.

"I am not a coward!"

He jumped onto Gus's back and sank his teeth into Gus's neck. Sharp needles of pain shot through Gus. He shook his neck, but Decker held on.

Moon Pie shrieked, "Get off him!"

"Hey, Moonie, what's all the commotion—"

Miss Lottie had stepped out of the bathroom. She stood in the doorway.

"Stop it, Decker! STOP IT RIGHT NOW!"

Miss Lottie ran and dove between them, landing on the floor with a loud thump. She grabbed Decker's collar and yanked him off Gus.

"STOP!" she yelled. She pushed Gus away with her free arm. He hit the doorjamb, yapped a sharp, pained bark, then scrambled to his feet so that he could look Decker right in the eye.

"You have to stop this," Gus said. His breathing was ragged. Warm blood trickled down his neck. "We're a pack—"

Decker lunged at him, his teeth barely missing Gus's ear.

"DECKER, NO!" Miss Lottie yanked him back by the collar.

Then Tank was there, with Roo at his side.

"What's going on?" Tank demanded.

Roo spun in circles, barking.

Miss Lottie held on to Decker's collar. Decker shook his head from side to side as spittle flew from his mouth. He wasn't making any words, only sounds. High-pitched, frantic sounds.

"This doesn't help anything," Gus said to him. "You've got to calm down—"

Decker snapped his jaws together, shook himself free from Miss Lottie, and leaped at Gus again, snarling.

"HEY!" cried Miss Lottie. She scrambled toward Decker on her hands and knees and reached over to grab him around his middle. "Do not hurt Gus!"

Moon Pie ran from side to side on the bed, barking.

"Miss Lottie, no! Don't grab him!" Moon Pie whimpered.

"Stop!" Tank growled.

Gus saw rage in Decker's eyes as Decker lunged toward him again.

"No, Decker, NO!" Miss Lottie yelled. She blocked Decker with her arm.

Decker was all teeth and fury. In a wild rage, his jaws clamped down on Miss Lottie's upper arm just hard enough to draw blood.

Miss Lottie's howl sounded strange and doglike. Her face crumpled as she looked up at the ceiling, wincing in pain.

"What have you done?" Gus asked.

"You're in for it now, Decker," Tank said.

Decker froze. The smell of his fear filled the room.

It smelled like a small, scared rabbit.

Miss Lottie reached for Decker's collar, but he snapped back to attention and dodged her hand. He spun around and raced down the hall. Gus wasn't sure where he thought he was running to, but he could hear from Decker's foot-falls that he was in a full gallop.

Roo flew after him. Seconds later she was back. "Decker's petrified," she said. "He ran into the laundry room to hide!"

Gus crept over to the door and stared down the hall. He could see the tip of Decker's tail poking out from behind a pile of clothes.

Miss Lottie was holding her upper arm with her hand. She struggled to get up. "You all stay!" she said to the pack. "Don't budge!"

She finally heaved herself up from the floor and tottered down the hall, holding the wall to steady herself. Without saying a word, she shut the door to the laundry room. She stood there for a moment before she lumbered back down the hall. She stared at them from the doorway.

"You poor, poor babies," she said, shaking her head. "How could I have been so blind?"

Gus

The rest of the night had been a blur. Pam, the neighbor, took care of Gus so that Miss Lottie could go to the hospital. At the emergency vet, they gave him four stitches, bandaged him up, and called him a lucky dog.

"He sure is," Pam said, shaking her head.

When he got home, he saw that Miss Lottie was also wrapped in bandages.

"Looks like we've been through a war," Miss Lottie said, laughing a bit. "Maybe we have."

Quinn was there. He knelt down and gently hugged Gus.

"Sorry you had to go through that," he whispered.

Gus leaned in and licked Quinn's cheek. Somehow Quinn knew the heartache of betrayal within a pack. He had seen what had happened with Decker and he knew, he just *knew.*

Pam put on her coat. "Let me know if you need me again. I'm right next door."

"Thanks, Pam," Miss Lottie said. "I don't know what I'd do without you and Quinn here." She threw an arm around Quinn and drew him toward her. "Remind me to thank your mom for letting you come over here so late. And for letting you look for the dogs all this time! You've been a real trooper."

"Thanks," Quinn said.

Pam paused at the door. "What time is he coming?"

"He said he'd be here in an hour," Miss Lottie said.

Pam fussed with the button on her coat. "Are you sure you don't need me?"

"I've got Quinn. We should be fine. But I'll let you know."

"Okay," Pam said. She paused. "It's the right thing."

Miss Lottie nodded. "It's still hard."

Gus didn't have to be told what would happen next. He knew.

When the doorbell rang, Gus didn't bark. Even Roo, who always went ballistic at the sound of the doorbell, only barked once.

"That's him," Miss Lottie said. She was sitting in the kitchen eating a dry piece of toast. Quinn rolled an empty water bottle on the kitchen table.

Miss Lottie took another bite, coughed, then rose from the table. It seemed to take her forever to get to the door.

The man she let in was tall and held a heavy leash. "Hey, Lottie." He nodded once. "Where is he?"

Miss Lottie brought the man to the laundry room, then came back into the kitchen and sat, staring out the window. She winced when she heard Decker's whimpering.

The man led Decker into the kitchen with a muzzle on. He looked like a different dog. His head hung low. His tail was firmly between his legs.

Gus felt his heart soften as he stared at the frightened dog. Decker had made life difficult for him, and yet Gus knew it wasn't really Decker's fault. Somewhere in his life he had experienced hurt and betrayal. Gus just hoped he could get past it with his new human.

"I've worked with plenty of dogs like him before," the man said. "He'll be fine."

"That's good to hear," Miss Lottie said. "As long as you don't have any other dogs there, he should be okay. He didn't mean to hurt *me*. He was going for Gus. I was stupid for getting in the middle of it all."

The man tugged on the leash. Decker sat obediently. "I'll work with him, then I'll find him a good home."

"Thanks for coming so late," Miss Lottie said. "I just—" She shrugged and shook her head. "I don't know."

"No problem," the man said. "I get it. You don't want to keep him locked up like that all night."

Miss Lottie wiped a tear away with the back of her hand and nodded. She bent down and rubbed Decker behind the ears. "You be good, you hear?"

Decker only looked at her. He smelled faintly of fear, but that was all.

Once Decker was gone, Miss Lottie let out a long sigh.

"I'm so sorry, you guys," she said. Her gaze settled on Tank. She went over and knelt next to his bed. "Especially you, buddy. I can't believe I blamed you." She rubbed him behind the ears. "I'm not sure what went on in the yard the other day, but I know now that it wasn't you."

After a moment, Tank rolled onto his back. Miss Lottie laughed. "Okay, I know what that means. Belly rub, coming right up!"

Gus

It was late. Tank and Gus sat on their beds, but they didn't lie down. Roo made dozens of circles on the rug in the middle of the room. Moon Pie, who had fought so hard to sleep in the big bed, squirmed in Miss Lottie's arms.

"You want to sleep here tonight?" she asked as she put him down. He hopped over to Tank and curled up next to him.

"Okey doke," Miss Lottie said. She turned off the overhead light but left a lamp on. "I'll leave a light on for you, Moonie. Good night, kiddos."

After she left, there was an uneasy silence.

"Is he really gone?" Moon Pie asked. "Really and truly?"

"Yes," Gus said. "Gone forever."

Roo stopped circling. She sat. "Why do you think he did

it?" she asked. "This is a good pack. This is a good home. Miss Lottie is a good human. I don't get it." She rose and started circling again.

"He was a bad dog," Tank said. He gently licked Moon Pie's tiny ear. Moon Pie yawned and snuggled in closer to Tank. "All those things, like good packs and good humans, aren't enough for bad dogs like him. They're greedy. They need more."

"I don't think so," Gus said. He trotted over to the couch to look for a tennis ball he had hidden there for safekeeping. "I think he didn't get any love when he was a pup."

"Oh, brother," Tank said.

"I mean it." Gus got down low and reached as far as he could under the sofa. "Got it!" He pulled the tennis ball toward him with his paw. It was perfect. Not too new, not too old. Plenty of springiness left in it, along with the good smells of beef and dirt. He splayed out on his bed with it between his paws.

"Love makes all the difference," he said.

Then, all at once, it hit him. His dog gift. All this time he had been wondering whether or not it was helpful. But after seeing how mean and bitter a dog could become without love, he realized that it was the most important gift he could have.

Love was, quite simply, everything.

Roo stopped circling. She wandered over to her bed and

plunked down onto it. "I'm just glad Decker's gone."

Gus smelled Ghost's odd, fishy scent. He looked up from his tennis ball.

"Gus . . . ," Moon Pie began.

"It's okay, Moon Pie." Gus rose. "Welcome, Ghost."

Ghost stood in the doorway, one paw held high, as if he wasn't sure whether to stay or dash out of the room.

"Come in," Gus said.

"That's okay," Ghost said. "I just wanted to be sure, well, you know . . ."

"He's gone," Gus said. "Thanks to you."

"And everyone's . . . ?"

"We're all fine. A little beat up, but we'll survive."

"Okay," Ghost said. He turned to leave.

"Ghost?"

"Yes?"

"You can come out and visit any time you'd like. Moon Pie won't mind." He glanced over at Moon Pie. "Right?"

Moon Pie paused. "Yeah. Sure."

Ghost swished his tail. "Maybe." He sauntered out of the room just as quietly as he had entered.

"You sure you're okay sleeping out here tonight, Moon Pie?" Gus asked. The small pug still looked a little shaken. "I bet Miss Lottie would love to have you."

Moon Pie blinked. "I'm okay here," he said. He put his head back down and closed his eyes.

But tomorrow Moon Pie would go back to Miss Lottie's comfy bed. He would get the best slices of meat off the cutting board. And all of them would be fine with that, because it was as it should be.

And if they were lucky, maybe Miss Lottie would sing along with her iPod, and Roo would join her, and they'd be one big, happy pack again.

Miss Lottie Before

After her husband died, Lottie wandered around her house a lot, staring outside, staring at photo albums, staring into space. Lost.

Nothing could fill the ache. Her macaroni and cheese tasted bland. She couldn't concentrate on her mystery novels. Everything on the television bored her.

She looked and she looked, but she couldn't find *it*, whatever *it* was. Sometimes it felt like this feeling, this word, this thing was on the tip of her tongue. If only she could remember it.

"Take up a hobby," her dear friend Gertie had said.

Miss Lottie tried, but her knitting was bumpy. Her clay pots were lopsided. Her paintings were splotchy.

The ache and the emptiness persisted.

So every day, she walked to the same spot and sat on the same bench under an oak tree. She would stay until darkness fell, only to come back the following morning. She didn't know what she thought about. Maybe nothing.

One day, instead of sitting under the oak, she decided to go to the pond. And there she saw a dog gnawing on a rock. A dog with a purpose. He stared at the ducks floating on the water. Like her, he seemed to be looking for something.

When Miss Lottie saw him, her heart beat faster. Then it swelled. This was *it*. That feeling, that word, that thing she had been looking for.

Family.

Epilogue

Six Months Later

Even though it was a sunny spring day at the dog park, with lots of good smells in the air and fat squirrels scurrying about, the pack was uneasy. Quinn had spread out a blanket and poured fresh water into bowls, but none of the pack looked interested in resting or water.

It had been six months since Decker had left, and the pack had finally, finally gone back to the way it used to be. Gus used his special dog gift daily, making sure they all felt loved and appreciated. He praised Tank for the way he helped Moon Pie with his nightmares. He calmed Roo when she started spinning too much. He cuddled with Moon Pie and gave him one of his Tiddle Widdle Chicken Bits each night. He gave the other one to Ghost, who had gone out of his way to help the pack, even though he would never admit it.

Every so often he would think of Decker. Of how he had acted the way he did because he didn't have enough love in his life. It was too late for Decker, but Gus knew his dog gift had made the rest of his pack feel happy and safe again.

"What if this new dog is just like . . . him?" Moon Pie asked. He sat on Quinn's lap, trembling.

"The chances are very slim," Gus said.

"Yes, but what if he IS?" Roo asked. "He could be, you know! He could be just as mean! What if he's mean and big and—"

"Roo, stop. I won't let it happen again. I promise," Gus said.

"Okaaaay . . ."

Miss Lottie's dented van pulled into the parking lot. The pack froze.

"They're here," Quinn said. He shaded his eyes with his hand as he watched Miss Lottie get out of the van.

Gus held his breath. As much as he had tried to reassure the pack, his real worry was that he might make the same mistake again. He hadn't listened to his deep-down dogginess before, and his pack had paid for it.

"Hey, everyone!" said Miss Lottie. She waved at them and opened the back door.

Gus watched closely as Miss Lottie reached into the

van. When she came out, she was carrying a small, shivery Yorkshire terrier. The spring breeze swept his sweet soapy scent toward Gus.

"Meet Percy!" said Miss Lottie.

Miss Lottie smiled and put Percy down on the ground. At first the small dog stayed close to her. But one gentle shove with Miss Lottie's foot, and he was off and running toward the pack. "Hey, everyone! I'm Percy! I just got a bath! I don't like baths, do you? I like playing tug-of-war most of all but sometimes I'll play catch. When I do play catch I don't always bring the ball back, but I think that's okay, don't you?"

Moon Pie wiggled in Quinn's lap.

"Go meet him, Moon Pie!" Quinn said. He pushed the little pug toward the new dog. It was clear that Moon Pie was thrilled that he was no longer the smallest member of the pack.

"I'm Moon Pie," he said. He puffed his chest out, took one step toward Percy, then glanced at Gus.

"Well, hi, Moon Pie! I like your name a lot," said Percy. He crouched down and sprang at Moon Pie. "I like the moon. And pies. Who doesn't like pies? Do you guys like pies? I do!"

Moon Pie didn't join in Percy's game. Gus suddenly realized that the pack was waiting for him. He had been so taken with the chatty little dog that he had forgotten his job.

"Looks okay to me," Tank said.

"He seems okay to me, too!" Roo said. "A little hyper, maybe—"

Percy was looking at Gus with big, dark eyes. He smelled of goodness and fairness and fun. He was exactly what the pack needed. Gus knew this. His deep-down dogginess was certain of it.

Gus gave his approval—one small woof and a quick wag.

"Hooray!" said Moon Pie. He danced in front of Percy, who wiggled his butt in the air and barked. Roo gave Percy a friendly nip before chasing him.

"Glad that's over with," Tank said. He chugged over to a sunny spot on the blanket and plopped down on it.

"Looks like they're all getting along!" Miss Lottie said. She dug around in one of the coolers until she found a bottle of water. She twisted the cap off, took a big gulp, and sat down next to Quinn. "How's the work going on the tree-house?" she asked.

"Good," said Quinn. "We're almost finished. Jessie's making the ladder for it right now."

"That's wonderful," Miss Lottie said. She took another gulp of water. "I bet you two will have lots of fun in it."

Gus wandered over to Quinn and sat down next to him. Quinn smiled.

"I've got something for you, Gus," he said. He dug into his backpack and pulled out a new tennis ball. "Go get it!"

Quinn tossed the ball to Gus, who jumped up and

caught it in midair. He jogged back to Quinn and dropped the ball by his feet.

"Nice job!" Quinn said. "Okay, let's see if you can get this one." He grunted as he threw the ball over a clump of trees. Gus watched the ball arc through the air before chasing it.

As soon as he turned the corner, he skidded to a stop.

He was there. Just a few feet away.

Decker.

An old man was sitting on a bench. Decker sat facing him with his chin resting on the old man's leg.

At first Gus wasn't sure if it was really him. He had gained weight. His coat looked thicker. And he was wagging his tail, something Gus had never seen him do before.

But his smell was what really struck Gus. He still had that strange, watery scent, but it was different now, more like a bowl of water that had been warmed by the sun.

"You're such a good boy, Decker," said the old man. He stroked Decker's ears. "A good, good boy."

Decker glanced over at Gus. He stopped wagging his tail and raised his head. He stared at Gus long and hard.

Gus tensed, but Decker only thumped his tail on the ground once, softly.

Gus dipped his head and wagged his tail.

So there *was* a good dog in Decker, buried deep inside the hard, frightened shell. That goodness just had to be let

out in a safe place where there was lots of love. Gus craved the liveliness of a big pack, but a pack of two was perfect for Decker. He could get the love he so desperately needed and not have to share.

Gus heaved a long, slow, contented sigh before grabbing the tennis ball in his teeth and running back to the others.

"This," said Miss Lottie, holding her arms up to the sky. "This is the kind of day dreams are made of. A perfect, perfect day."

Gus dropped the ball and trotted over to her. He nestled into her lap, which he hadn't done in ages. He felt the

perfectness of the day, too, the kind of day they had both been waiting for, and wanted to share it with her.

Tank wandered over to them, then Roo, then Moon Pie. They all snuggled around her. Percy hesitated, then curled up next to Moon Pie.

Miss Lottie reached over and held Quinn's hand.

"Do you feel it, Quinn?" She closed her eyes and took a deep breath. "The perfectness of this day?"

Quinn blushed. "I do," he said quietly.

Gus sighed. It wasn't just the perfectness of the day, with its soft breezes and springtime scents, although that was part of it.

Gus knew that what they were really feeling, right then and there, on that perfect, warm, spring afternoon, was love.

Acknowledgments

I'm so grateful to be part of a brilliant and supportive pack of writers who read draft after draft of this book. As always, big tail wags and slurpy kisses to Sarah Aronson, Brenda Ferber, Jenny Meyerhoff, and Laura Ruby. I couldn't do it without you guys!

Huge thanks to Stephanie Fretwell-Hill, my agent and fairy godmother, whose doggedness gave me hope at a time when I really needed it. Thank you, thank you, thank you for all your hard work on my behalf.

And to Kristin Daly Rens, the most amazing and warm-hearted editor a writer could ever ask for. You made this book so much better with your wise and insightful comments. Thank you for gently pushing me to dig deeper. Your dog gift is love!